Austin certainly had Laney's attention as he sauntered toward her.

Tux unbuttoned, black bow tie gone and black Stetson on. He stopped only a few feet away, and in the stable's dim halo of yellowish light, his expression was unreadable, yet tantalizing.

"I've been wanting to talk to you all night."

She touched her hair, styled into an elegant updo for the party, as his rich tenor swirled over her.

"Talk to me? About what?"

His eyes swaggered over her from head to toe, lingering here and there in places that caused her skin to warm.

"Your choice of attire for the gala," he stated matter-of-factly.

Not sure if Austin was teasing or not, Laney met his gaze head-on. "What's wrong with it?" she blurted out.

Austin shook his head. "It's different from your usual T-shirt and jeans," he stated, without a hint of a smile. "And on you, that gown is far too stunning to ignore."

Books by Harmony Evans

Harlequin Kimani Romance

Lesson in Romance
Stealing Kisses
Loving Laney

HARMONY EVANS

is an award-winning author for Harlequin Kimani Romance, the leading publisher of African-American romance. She is the recipient of the 2013 Romance Slam Jam Emma Award for Debut Author of the Year. In addition, she was a 2012 RT Reviewers' Choice Awards double finalist (First Series Romance and Kimani Romance). She is also a member of Romance Writers of America.

Harmony is a single mom to a beautiful, too-smart-for-her-own-good daughter who makes her grateful for life daily. Her hobbies include cooking, baking, knitting, reading and, of course, napping. Her favorite place to visit is New York City. Her biggest dream is to someday live and write in Paris, France. Currently, she resides in Cleveland, Ohio, home of the Rock and Roll Hall of Fame!

Be sure to connect with Harmony on your favorite social media network!

Harmony Evans

Loving
LANEY

HARLEQUIN® KIMANI™ ROMANCE

I would like to dedicate this book to moms everywhere. We have the
most important job in the world. Stay strong!

Recycling programs
for this product may
not exist in your area.

ISBN-13: 978-0-373-86357-0

LOVING LANEY

Copyright © 2014 by Jennifer Jackson

HARLEQUIN®

Printed in U.S.A.   ™ www.Harlequin.com

Dear Reader,

There's something about wide-open spaces and small towns that inspire romance. Throw a superrich family, a surprise pregnancy and blackmail into the mix and you have all the fixings for a juicy scandal.

Equestrian Laney Broward is still basking in the glow of her gold medal win when millionaire horse breeder Austin Johns surprises her with a passionate New Year's Eve kiss that turns into an all-night lovemaking session. When Laney becomes pregnant, she fears the stigma of being a single mom, and worries about disappointing the entire Broward family and losing her independence.

Austin Johns isn't used to being tied down to anyone or anything except his prizewinning thoroughbreds. Now that he's going to be a daddy, he's willing to happily take on the responsibility. But will Laney let him?

Loving Laney, the third novel in the Browards of Montana series, is a story you will never forget.

Be blessed,

Harmony Evans

Prologue

Dallas, Texas: New Year's Eve

I've never seen anything so ridiculous, thought Laney Broward as she watched her friends openly fawn over Austin Johns. For almost the entire evening, Mara and Robyn had been taking turns narrating a play-by-play of his every move.

She glanced around the enormous room crowded with men and women kicking up their heels and tossing back drinks as they danced the night away to a live band.

Hundreds of glittering snowflakes were suspended from the ceiling supported by huge Greek-style columns wrapped in shimmery silver brocade. Round tables draped in white tulle with gray organza bows surrounded the perimeter, each topped with miniature candelabra where ivory candles provided a romantic glow in the dimly lit room.

It was the perfect setting for a New Year's Eve gala. The effect was magical, mystical and filled with the promise of something special. Then why did Laney feel so out of place?

"What's he doing now?" Robyn asked, craning her neck like an ostrich.

"Oh, he's just being gorgeous," Mara reported with a giggle.

Laney rolled her eyes. "I think that's the worst line I've ever heard. I hope you weren't going to use that one."

Mara's face fell momentarily and then immediately lit up. "I think he's headed this way!" she exclaimed.

Laney planted herself in front of them, blocking their view.

"Both of you have been around horses too long," she admonished. "Austin is just a man. He walks and talks and eats just like we do."

Her friends, who had competed with her on equestrian teams throughout her career before Laney won the gold medal, stared at her like she was crazy. Both had consumed a fair amount of champagne, while Laney had been nursing the same glass of bubbly for over an hour.

"Well, at least we recognize perfection when we see it," Robyn scolded.

Mara raised her glass. "I'll drink to that!" she slurred.

Laney turned away slightly, refusing to concede to their good-humored jab. She eyed an oversize clock that hung just above the ballroom doors. It was thirty minutes to the "Big Kiss Moment" and she was dateless.

Worst, she had to be on her best behavior. On New Year's Eve, no less! Not that she would have done anything really crazy. Her reputation was sound and she wanted it to stay that way.

Ever since Laney had won a gold medal, the media frenzy had been glowing—and rabid. For a while she basked in the attention, as any sane person would, but she also knew how quickly the media could turn from being your best friend to your worst enemy. She just didn't want it to happen at a gala event sponsored by Austin, or anyone else for that matter.

Laney's stomach knotted as she quickly scanned the perimeter of the room. There was no telling if or where the paparazzi were hiding. She was on high alert and not taking any chances. There was no way she was going to ring in the new year as the subject of one of those tacky celebrity viral videos. Laney took a sip of her lukewarm drink and almost gagged. "No man is perfect," she scoffed, turning back to face her friends.

"Really?" Robyn accused, placing one hand on her hip. "You'd have to be a horse's you-know-what not to see that Austin is the epitome of every woman's dream."

"Not me," she insisted. "I barely know the man."

A true statement, although it wasn't like she'd never met Austin. On several occasions, he'd been out to the BWB, the Broward family ranch located in Granger, Montana, to conduct business with Laney's mother, Gwendolyn. They'd also run into each other in London during the Olympics.

Mara peered down her nose at Laney. "You don't have to know the man to appreciate, and take advantage of, everything he has to offer."

Laney stifled a mocking laugh. Both times she'd seen Austin, he hadn't given her anything more than a polite handshake and some friendly conversation. And she was supposed to take advantage of him? She might be dateless, but she wasn't desperate.

One thing Laney did know about Austin, and did not appreciate, was his reputation as a ladies' man. He ran through women like a wild stallion galloping through endless prairie grass. Tongues wagged that his conquests were as global as his appetite for travel: Paris, Barcelona, Rome.

But as far as she knew, no one in the little town of Granger had been able to saddle him—even for one night.

Laney pursed her lips to stifle a fierce retort. Defending herself to her friends would only lead to an argument, which was no way to end what had been a very successful year for the trio.

"Just look, Laney," Robyn implored with a nudge of her elbow. "Start with his body, and go from there."

"As if you'd want to go anywhere else," Mara added with a wicked smile.

Laney tensed when Mara put her hands on her shoulders, forcing her to turn around and admit to herself what every other woman in the room already knew: Austin Johns was the most handsome man at the ball.

Her heart did a little skip as she watched Austin weave his way through the crowded dance floor. When he paused, the women gravitated toward him and the men just wanted to shake his hand, perhaps hoping some of the "Austin mojo" would rub off on them.

The millionaire horse breeder took all the attention in stride, as if he were just out for a stroll rather than combing through a sea of gyrating bodies. At about six feet three inches tall, he towered over all the women and many of the men. Laney cast her head over her shoulder toward her friends. They were both wearing I-told-you-so grins, but she wasn't about to give them the satisfaction that they were right all along.

A waiter swung past with an empty tray and she handed him her champagne flute.

"I'm going to get some fresh air. Why don't you two

go out on the dance floor and mingle before we all turn back into pumpkins?"

"As long as Prince Charming is there to whisk me away into his carriage, I'm there," Mara announced, kicking off her shoes. "C'mon, Robyn."

Laney watched her friends get swallowed up into a line dance. They stumbled frequently, like two colts trying to get a sense of the ground. It was a comical sight and she found herself smiling, in spite of her cautious mood.

Prince Charming. There's no such thing.

"Especially in Montana," she muttered as she walked through the estate's massive foyer. Being single definitely had its challenges in Big Sky Country, where there were more cattle per square foot of land than eligible men. Laney was thankful she had her horses to keep her mind off the lack of suitable dating options and she looked forward to returning home to Granger tomorrow.

Right now, though, she had to get through tonight.

After a quick visit to the ladies' room, Laney hurried outside to the place where she felt most comfortable— no matter what city, state or country she happened to be visiting at the moment—the stables.

Earlier in the evening, Austin, the primary sponsor of the evening's gala, had used the stable to unveil his plans for a new therapeutic riding center in Dallas. Laney and her friends had arrived late to the event and had missed his presentation, so she was eager to learn more. Now was as good a time as any to get a sneak peek.

She rubbed her bare arms as she followed the paved driveway around the estate. While it rarely snowed in Dallas, the evening's low temperature was a chilly reminder to its inhabitants that it very well could.

Laney arrived at the stable moments later. It wasn't far from the main house and the evening's festivities were amplified through strategically placed outdoor speakers. She heard the lead singer from the band loudly informing the crowd that there were only ten more minutes to midnight. When she looked back, she saw that the ballroom doors were open and guests mingled outside on the stone terrace, chattering and laughing.

Eager for peace and quiet, Laney tugged on the service door of the stable and slipped inside. As she eased it closed, she breathed in deeply and smiled.

They were all here. The odors of pungent earth, of crisp hay and alfalfa, of sawdust and pine, of leather and oil. Real. Tangible. A part of the air, a part of her.

As a child, the gentle eyes of the horses had wooed her. She'd fallen in love and never looked back. In the stables, she didn't have to hide. Not even from herself.

"It's about time you showed up."

The voice had the slow, easy drawl of a cowboy. None too hurried, and always sexy.

Laney heard her shocked breath whistle through her teeth. She blinked in the low light, but couldn't see anyone. She took a step back and placed her hand on the door, ready to book at any moment.

"Austin?"

Seconds later, she heard a teasing chuckle and a neigh of disapproval.

"Don't pout, Sadie, I'll be back to check on you in the morning," Austin soothed. He emerged from a large stall at the far end of the stable. "But right now, I must see why this beautiful young lady has been ignoring me all night."

She let go of the doorknob. "How did you know I was here?"

Austin shrugged. "I didn't exactly, but I figured if you were going anywhere on the grounds, it would be to the stables. I knew you couldn't ignore me here."

Ignoring him? *Lord knows I've tried,* she thought.

But Austin certainly had Laney's attention now as he sauntered toward her. Tux unbuttoned and flaps secured behind hands stuck in his pockets. The black bowtie gone and the black Stetson on. He stopped only a few feet away and in the dim halo of yellowish-light cast by the fixtures above their heads, his expression was unreadable, yet tantalizing.

"You scared me!" she managed to whisper, not wanting to disturb the horses. "I thought you were some crazy journalist sneaking around wanting to take my picture."

Austin squared his hands like a makeshift camera against his eyes and peered through them. "Say cheese."

Laney's heart raced against her will under his pretend lens. To be the subject of Austin's "admiration" was the dream of most of the women in Granger, and likely all of the females at the party, but not her.

"How about I say goodbye?" she fumed under his intense gaze. She wasn't mad at him, but her reaction to him confused her. His eyes seemed to burn a hole through her long-held image of him as a business associate of her mother's.

He dropped his hands to his massive chest. "Whoa, girl. I've been wanting to talk to you all night. You can't leave yet."

As his rich tenor swirled over her, Laney knew she would never tire of hearing his voice.

She touched her hair, styled into an elegant updo for the party. "Talk to me? About what?" she asked, trying not to sound flattered.

His eyes swaggered over her from head to toe, lingering here and there in places that caused her skin to warm.

"Your choice of attire for the gala," he stated matter-of-factly.

She froze and her mouth dropped open. First Austin unwittingly scared her and now he was openly judging her.

"Two minutes to midnight, folks!"

She ignored the singer's gleeful warning and smoothed her hands along the side of her royal blue full-length gown. This wasn't some department store knock-off, but rather it was custom designed for her. Not because she was a Broward and could afford it, but because she wanted to remain true to herself: one-of-a-kind. Unique. And right now, steaming mad.

Not sure if Austin was teasing or not, Laney met his gaze head-on. "What's wrong with it?" she blurted.

Austin shook his head. "It's far too different than your usual T-shirt and jeans," he stated, without a hint of a smile.

How dare he insult me, Laney thought. As a child, her brothers, Wes and Jameson, had teased her relentlessly about her tomboyish wardrobe and the memories came flooding back. Now that she was older, she knew they hadn't meant to hurt her, but the pain was still there.

Just as she was about to tell Austin where he could stuff his unwanted opinions, he tilted his Stetson back slightly with the tip of his thumb.

"And on you, that gown is far too stunning to ignore."

10…9…8…

Was it the music or her heart that suddenly stopped as Austin stepped closer and draped his hands on her bare shoulders?

7…6…5…

Austin seemed not to hear the drum roll or the guests chanting the countdown. He tilted her chin up and she stared at his lips, slightly bewildered.

4…3

She'd never been this close to Austin, never smelled his rough, masculine scent, never dreamed she'd want to be even closer.

…2…

Laney closed her eyes, suddenly aware that she wanted to grasp onto something she wasn't even sure was going to happen, but a part of her hoped that it would. The part that foretold regret.

…1…

Austin cradled her face in his hands and lowered his mouth to hers.

"Happy New Year, Laney."

Ignoring all sense and logic, amid the fireworks and distant gun shots, she slipped her hands around his waist and caved into the spell of his kiss. He was gentle at first, exploring the edges, feathering the center, his movements tugging at long-buried desire. The nerve points of her mouth jolted awake, as if from a deep sleep, reminding her of how much she'd missed the touch of a man's lips. Now the feel of Austin's lips was branded upon her senses forever.

Their embrace was like a blanket they huddled underneath against the clamor of noisemakers and strains of "Auld Lang Syne." They owned the dark, the passion and the promise.

The old was made new. And when Austin lifted his mouth from hers, she felt more than sudden, unexpected desire. There was also the innate fear that she might never be kissed that way by Austin again, and the excitement that maybe she would.

She bit her lip, plumper now from his kisses.

He tipped his hat, bowing slightly and her heart fell when he started to walk away.

Her independent spirit willed her not to run to him, while at the same time her caring nature compelled her not to disturb the horses she loved so much.

She dropped her voice to a whisper. "Where are you going?" she called out.

He turned around and seemed unperturbed by what had just occurred between them. His world was unshaken, while hers tilted crazily on its axis.

"Home."

Laney arched a brow. She knew Austin had a large estate that included two huge stables just outside of Dallas. But she couldn't just let him leave, at least not until she found out why he had kissed her.

"Now? But what about the party? Aren't you a sponsor?"

Austin nodded, and then chuckled. "I think the festivities will go on without me."

He was moving away from her again, easing toward the door, away from something he had started.

She took a few hurried steps and managed to tap his shoulder before quickly drawing back. It was hard and muscular under the black cloth of his tux.

"You probably shouldn't be driving," she advised.

"It's New Year's Eve and it could be dangerous on the roads."

Austin folded his arms and smiled. "Don't worry about me, I'm staying close tonight."

"Really? Where?" she asked, for once not caring if she sounded overly curious.

Austin pushed open the service door and leaned against it. "A couple of years ago, I sold the owners of this estate two of my best thoroughbreds, both of which have made them a ton of money recently on the circuit. In exchange, there's a little cottage on the grounds and they let me stay in it."

"Wow. That's really nice. Much better than a hotel."

He nodded and there was a sudden gleam in his eye. "Yeah, it comes in handy those times when I've partied a little too hard. But I've been good tonight."

Laney thought back to the lukewarm champagne and smiled. "Me, too."

He raised an eyebrow. "Well, in that case, would you like to see it?"

Although she didn't know Austin very well, he wasn't a total stranger. He was a friend of the Browards and highly regarded by her mother, Gwen. Still she knew it was crazy to go with him. But something inside her wanted to go against the grain of her own personal conventions. It was, after all, New Year's Eve.

She let her eyes travel across Austin's broad shoulders. If she couldn't be in his bed, she had the odd wish to be positioned under it, hidden from view. She wanted to listen to him breathe and feel the weight of his body dangerously close to hers.

She looked into Austin's eyes and nodded her answer. *What would Mara and Robyn think?* she thought.

They'd be jealous as all get out.

Laney hid a brief smile as they emerged into the chilly air. She hitched up her dress slightly and followed him down a wide dirt path.

The sky was clear and brilliant with stars and the temperature seemed to drop even more as they walked. By the time they arrived at the little home, which was located adjacent to a large pasture, she was shivering.

Laney rubbed her bare shoulders and read the hand-carved sign on the door. "'Shepherd's Cottage.' Cute name. What does it mean?"

She stepped inside and Austin closed and locked the door behind them.

"This place was built a long time ago for people hired to mind the cattle. If they didn't want to go home, they could sleep here. Since this ranch is now primarily used for breeding and raising horses, the owners use it as a guest house."

She rubbed her bare shoulders again and shivered when Austin ran his hands down her arms. Her skin immediately goose-pimpled under his gentle touch while his reassuring smile warmed her in places his eyes couldn't see.

"I'm sorry it's so cold in here. It will only take me a minute to get the fireplace going."

He shrugged out of his tuxedo jacket and helped her into it. "In the meantime, you can wear this."

His jacket was way too big, but it was warm. She wrapped it around her body and inhaled the hint of spicy cologne that came with it.

"Make yourself comfortable."

She nodded and took a few steps forward. As she

looked around, she realized that the cottage had only one room.

On her left, fairly close to the door, there was a sitting area facing the fireplace, a galley kitchen with a breakfast nook and a door she assumed led to the bathroom. The white-washed walls held various pen-and-ink drawings of landscapes, horses and mountains.

She pivoted to the right and spotted a small alcove with two steps leading up to an old-fashioned iron bed, covered in a thick ivory satin duvet.

Cozy was one word that came to mind.

The other caused her to bite her lip. She quickly turned back toward the living area. Austin was down on one knee, tending to the fire. The muscles beneath his shirt rippled under the white fabric as he arranged the kindling and the logs. Her breath caught in her throat as he struck a match and set the wood aflame.

But it wasn't until Austin stood up, grasped his Stetson with one hand and placed it on a peg by the front door in one fell swoop, that she lost it. To her, that simple gesture meant that he was home, and just for tonight, she was right here with him.

"Why did you kiss me?" she blurted.

"I don't know," he admitted, rubbing the back of his neck. "Why did you kiss me back?"

Laney opened her mouth, as if an explanation would simply form without any thought. Kissing Austin back wasn't that simple. Neither was the reason.

She shrugged, a little too hard, and his tux jacket fell to the floor.

"I think we both need to find out," he said, approaching her. "Don't you?"

His low voice, a rich undercurrent to the pop and hiss of the kindling, made her knees shake.

A moment later, Laney felt herself nod, so intrigued by him that she found herself holding her breath as he unbuttoned his shirt.

He shed it quickly, not saying a word, not inviting her to look away. Somehow he knew that her eyes had been opened to something that needed to be explored.

The white T-shirt he wore cloaked those muscles that she knew were always there but could never touch. When he stood in front of her, so tantalizingly close, she couldn't help herself. She reached out and ran a finger down the middle of his abdomen. The ridges there were tight and hard, yet pulsed with barely contained energy.

He groaned and his hands grasped her waist as he pulled her against him. At once, she pressed her lips firmly against his neck and froze, plying his salty skin with her tongue, while his fingers deftly manipulated the zipper of her evening gown. It slid to the floor and Austin stepped back, yet not so far that she couldn't see the well of desire in his dark eyes as they swept over her lace bra and panties.

The answers they sought lay in the crackle of wood and the gentle hush of their breathing, yet for a moment, neither moved.

Austin took a step back, hesitating now, but Laney pulled him back, not willing to let him go.

For reasons she didn't fully comprehend, she needed to know him. She needed to feel this. His hard length, still clothed, rolling against her bare stomach. She weaved her body against him until he grunted and threaded his fingers in her long hair. He kissed her deeply, his tongue on a mission with no map. She was his guide, opening herself to him, allowing him to drink of her, knowing innately that he would never be satisfied, wanting him to keep on needing.

His mouth worked down her neck, his fingers twisting in her bra straps, kneading her shoulders, unhooking her bra. That male energy pulsed tight against her, making her yearn to take him in her mouth, to feel that energy spread through her body.

He lifted his lips and his hands spanned her bare back, drawing her even closer to him, and her nipples rubbed against his bare chest.

Laney moaned and Austin lifted her up in his arms. She allowed herself to be carried by him, not fighting the primal urge to be dominated by this man.

She wanted this.

Although they couldn't voice it to each other, deep down they had a common goal: to discover and to forget.

Austin laid her gently on the bed and she watched with wide eyes as he unzipped his trousers. Eased off his briefs. At the sight of him, she gasped. The length, wide as a river; smooth as glass on top, hard as a rock underneath, power coursing through unbidden. Her mouth began to water and she reached for him. Austin lay upon her, his smile almost imperceptible, his body elongated and seemed to never end. In the firelight, his skin was dark bronze, moist with sweat, firm with muscle. She trailed her fingers down his back and over his round buttocks and spread her legs in anticipation.

Their lips ground together again, tongues darting and playing, as they both sought to prolong their desire and their time together.

Austin's fingers tweaked one of her nipples and she

writhed beneath him, wanting more of his touch and more of him.

Sensing her need, he ended the kiss, cupped her breasts and lapped at her large nipples until they were hard. She looked down at the wet, swollen peaks and bit her bottom lip, as Austin pursed his lips and gently blew them dry.

Moving downward, Austin tongued her belly button, making her laugh. Her giggles quickly turned into gasps as he kissed her inner thighs, causing her muscles to quiver uncontrollably.

Laney moaned as his tongue hungrily darted across her skin, swirled briefly into her wet core, and out again, landing firmly on her ultra-sensitive pearl. Like a marionette on an invisible string, his gentle lips controlled her, beckoning her to buck. It only took a few moments and when she did, the satin sheets rolled underneath them. She cried out, fisting and clutching at the duvet, now a stage, barely able to contain her ecstatic agony.

After protecting them, Austin laid upon her once more, grunting low, murmuring softly in her ear. As he slowly, so slowly, inserted his length into her, she squeezed her eyes shut, her mouth going slack.

Laney opened her eyes and Austin stilled above her, breathing heavily, his arms stock-straight, palms flat against the mattress. The firewood shifted with a loud hiss, but neither of them flinched. His dark eyes gazed into hers and she bit her lip again at what she saw in them. No more a calm river, but a whirlpool of lust.

He began to move inside her so rapidly that she brought her hands to his massive shoulders, afraid she would fall off the bed. She tried to palm them, but gave up and settled on his shoulder blades. When she found a spot, she held on, like a mountain climber grasping sheer, slick rock, never letting go, never looking down, for fear of dying.

Her hair fell down around her face and she thrashed her head from side to side, moaning. She opened her legs wider, so Austin could climb higher, bore deeper.

He impaled her as his own, over one erotic threshold and then another, scaling and moving together, until she cried out again, desperate for more.

The freedom Austin was giving her, those undulating waves that were no match against fear, taking her outside of herself as their mutual pleasure rose to almost unbearable heights.

"Don't hold back, Laney," he urged, breathing hard. He found her lips and groaned. "Because I can't."

His neck corded as he slammed into her one last time and lifted his face to the sky. His chin jutting forth, eyes squeezed shut, as he froze in place.

Laney opened and closed her legs around his waist, and then finally locked them around his slick body. She moved her hips greedily to claim every drop that poured forth.

Emptying him.

Filling her.

So forbidden, so wanton, so unbelievably good.

The fire continued to crackle, and the beads of sweat that rolled from their bodies did not dampen their desire. No longer uncertain and not wanting to waste another moment, Laney and Austin began to eagerly explore each other again. Neither one considered, nor cared, what the new year would bring.

Chapter 1

"It was the kiss that changed everything," Laney whispered.

Stella Rose nuzzled her neck. Named after her favorite lead character from the play *A Streetcar Named Desire,* and her favorite flower, Stella Rose was Laney's prized thoroughbred and her closest confidante.

"Not yours, silly," Laney exclaimed, giggling. "Austin's!"

She gently patted Stella's chestnut mane. "Only you know how I truly feel about him," she whispered. "That's a secret between us girls."

Her newly minted sister-in-law, Brooke, who'd married Laney's older brother Jameson, knew the biggest secret of all.

Laney was four months pregnant with Austin's child.

All because of one night that she would never forget.

Ever since New Year's Eve, Austin was the focus of her dreams, and they were naughty indeed. So much so, she'd often wake up in a sweat and it was difficult to control her thoughts for the remainder of the day.

But if she were honest with herself, the fact was that on most days she didn't know how she felt about Austin. Only that she was scared to tell him the truth. First, she had to get through the process of telling her family.

"I sure wish they were as easy to talk to you as you are, Stella." She grabbed the leather reins. "Come on, girl. Let's get you groomed before you get as antsy as I am."

Laney's boots made a sucking sound as she led the horse through the pasture. Spring and early summer was rainy season in Montana. It was great for the soil and the vegetation, but terrible for her long, straight hair, which she kept tucked up under her taupe cowboy hat to try to avoid the frizzies.

When she reached the rough-hewn log fence, she leaned against it and took in the blessings before her eyes.

She had her own home on the huge Broward family homestead, complete with a large stable and plenty of pasture for her horses to graze. The white square-shaped clapboard farmhouse, circa 1930, was just the right size and suited her ideal of "organized simplicity." Beyond, prairie grasses swayed gently as far as she could see. Farther still, a ridge of mountains jutted against the blue sky.

But it was the air she loved the most. Breathe in clean, fresh Montana air and everything seemed right again. At least for a little while.

Laney unhitched the fence gate and led Stella Rose out of the paddock. She was almost inside the barn when she heard tires crunching on the long gravel driveway.

She looked up and saw Brooke approaching. Everyone she knew in Granger had a truck or an SUV and at least one horse. Brooke had all three, plus a Jeep, the vehicle that she was slowly driving into the clearing just to the left of the stable.

"Hey," Laney called out, patting her waist. Even though she was wearing jeans one size larger, she was oddly relieved that there was barely a bulge. It had become a habit to check and she was glad to know that even this far along, she still wasn't showing.

Keeping a firm grip on the reins, she drew Stella Rose to one side and patted her nose with her other hand to calm her. Although with her ranch hands coming and going, the horse was used to cars in close proximity, Laney wasn't taking any chances. Horses startled easily, sometimes for reasons that only they knew.

Brooke exited the car. "Hay is for horses," she quipped, tossing her long curls over her shoulder.

Laney rolled her eyes. "Ha-ha. You creative types have the corniest sense of humor."

Brooke, in jeans and an oversize yellow button-down shirt with a clay stain on it, put her hands on her slim hips. "That reminds me. Did I ever tell you the one about the elderly printmaker and the nude model?"

Laney held up her hand. "No, and please don't. I'm pregnant, remember? My stomach is very sensitive."

She loosened the cinch that secured the saddle. "Now enough with the jokes. Come help me get Stella Rose settled. She and I just finished a nice ride. It'll be our last…until the baby comes."

At the thought of not riding her horses for another five months, something welled up in her throat. The further along she got in her pregnancy, the more risks there were with riding, and at her last visit, her doctor had ordered her to stop.

Her eyes burned with tears and she turned so Brooke couldn't see her face as she led Stella Rose away.

Riding was her life, and although the safety of her baby was her number one priority now, the sacrifice still hurt. She just needed some time to get used to it.

Back in the stall, Brooke's hazel eyes flitted down to her abdomen. Laney wanted to squirm with unease. She guessed she'd have to get used to people looking at her stomach all the time, too.

She led Stella Rose into her stall, unbridled her and put on her halter.

Brooke followed. "Is everything okay? I haven't seen you in a while and I've been worried."

Laney took off Stella Rose's cinch and hung it on a hook outside the stall, warming at the sentiment. Her initial reaction to Brooke's sudden marriage to Jameson had not been positive. However, she'd lived up to her role as the "neutral" and "quiet" one in the Broward family and had not said a word.

Now she was glad she hadn't voiced her opinion. If she had, she and Brooke would not be on their way to becoming good friends.

Laney nodded. "Yes, I saw my OB-GYN last week and he says everything looks good."

"I'll say it is. You're not even showing yet," Brooke said, admiringly.

For Laney, not showing early in her pregnancy was a blessing. It had given her some time to try to figure things out, without her family poking their noses into her life. Unfortunately, her answers only led to more difficult questions. One of which was how in the world was she going to raise her child alone?

"*Yet* is the operative word," Laney emphasized. "The doctor says I could start to pop at any time."

"Even so, I hope when I get pregnant, I'll be as lucky and as beautiful as you are."

Laney blushed and laughed. "Thanks. And I'm hoping to be an auntie sooner, rather than later."

Brooke looked away, as if she were embarrassed. "I'll get back to you on that. Jameson and I are just enjoying being a married couple right now. Throwing children into the mix would only complicate things."

"Tell me about it," Laney muttered.

In an instant, she felt ashamed at her statement. Although she was starting to get more excited about the baby as the days went on, she still felt guilty about keeping the little one a secret from her family for so long.

As for Austin, he was too busy traveling the world to even care about what was happening with her, not to mention the town of Granger.

Just last week, her father, Steven Broward, the most powerful man in Granger and one of the wealthiest in the state, mentioned that he had emailed Austin a few newspaper articles about all the land grabbing that was going on in Granger. Laney wasn't at all surprised that her father had yet to receive a response.

Of course, Laney knew that not answering an email did not mean that Austin was unfit to be a parent. That would be ludicrous. But it did speak volumes about how easy it was for Austin to ignore her father, even though he had conducted business with the Broward family.

Or maybe Austin was trying to send the message that the Browards themselves didn't matter, neither did the land grabbers and least of all, Laney. Although he'd contacted her a few times the week after their evening together, she hadn't heard from him since.

Laney took off Stella Rose's saddle and handed it to Brooke.

"I'm sorry. That didn't come out right. I'm happy about the baby. It's just that—"

"Nobody can blame you for being upset," Brooke interrupted. She wiped the saddle down with a towel before placing it on a shelf. "You're going to be a single mom. That's a situation that would be difficult for anyone to face."

Laney took off the saddle blanket. It was a little damp from the ride, so she hung it over the stall door to dry.

She sighed. "Yeah. I'm dealing with things the best I can."

In truth, Laney was scared to death, but she tried not to think about it. If she did, she would never be able to gain enough courage to tell her family.

Laney grabbed a clean towel off a hook and started to wipe the saddle marks off Stella Rose's back.

Brooke frowned. "Where's Trey? Do you really have to do all this work?"

Trey Dawson, Laney's equine manager, was in charge of running the stable and taking care of her seven horses. He also assisted with her breeding program, everything from fielding calls from interested buyers to monitoring test tubes.

Laney walked around Stella so she could rub down her other side. "He has the morning off. Besides, I can still groom my horses. It relaxes me. And Stella Rose is special to me."

Stella Rose, the foal of Daphne Blue and Dante's Inferno, both champions, was a beautiful chestnut thoroughbred. As her beloved horse had grown to adulthood, Laney had gotten closer and closer to her until one day she'd decided that she would never sell her or breed her. After her gold medal win, Stella was officially retired and seemed perfectly content to spend her days grazing and eating.

Laney raised an eyebrow. "You may not be a horse breeder, but you're a rancher, just like I am. Do you mean to tell me that when you get pregnant, you're going to stop being who are?"

Brooke paused. "I may be a rancher, but my heart is in being an artisan. When I have a baby, I certainly wouldn't stop doing pottery."

Laney pointed her towel at Brooke. "That's what I'm talking about. Women don't have to change who they are just to have a baby."

Brooke nodded in agreement. "You're right. I'm just worried about you, that's all. When you told me you thought you'd had a miscarriage early on in your pregnancy, I—"

Laney wiped Stella Rose's face, ignoring her neigh of disapproval. "Well, I didn't," she stated firmly. "I was mistaken and I'm fine."

Brooke cocked her head to the side. "I wouldn't expect anything less from a gold medalist," she teased, trying to lighten the mood.

Laney laughed and tossed the towel into a basket outside the stall to be washed later. She started to check Stella Rose's hooves for any rocks or pebbles that may have gotten in them during their ride.

"Where do you keep that thing anyway? Hidden in some hay?" Brooke asked. She looked around, pretending like she was on a hunt to find Laney's gold medal.

Laney cast a secretive smile. "Don't worry. It's in a very safe place."

Satisfied that her horse was appropriately groomed, she undid the halter. Both women laughed when Stella Rose immediately started nibbling at the hay pile in the corner.

They exited the stall and Laney secured the latch. Stella Rose's ears pricked up at the sound.

"Don't worry, sweetheart," Laney cooed lovingly. "When Trey gets back in a little while, he'll put you out in the pasture with everyone else. You need some time to cool down now, okay?"

Stella Rose stared at her owner and then dipped her head back down to her food.

Brooke giggled. "Good thing I speak horse, too. Otherwise—"

"You'd think I was crazy?"

Brooke nodded. "I haven't gotten to the point where I talk to my pottery," she joked. "And I hope I never will!"

They both roared with laughter as they walked outside.

"So, did you find anything out from Jameson? What's the deal with the family meeting?"

Brooke pulled her hair back in a loose ponytail. "Other than more talk about the land-grabbers in Granger, he doesn't know."

Leave it to Jameson to have his head buried in the ground, Laney thought. Her brother wouldn't know gossip if it hit him in the face.

"I bet Jameson will be the first one at the meeting," Laney said wryly. "We both know how he feels about strangers buying up our town."

Brooke nodded. "He's a real hometown boy. He loves ranching and the town of Granger so much."

"You know that better than anyone," Laney replied.

Brooke's family, the Palmers, were ranchers, too, but certainly not at the same level as the Browards, both land and profitwise.

She still couldn't believe Jameson had married Brooke just so that she could keep her half of the family ranch. Due to an odd codicil in Brooke's father's will, Brooke had to be married to inherit her half of Palmer Ranch. And even though Brooke had no real interest in ranch life, she had felt compelled to carry out her father's wishes.

Laney adored the BWB Heritage Ranch, the formal name for the Browards' massive estate, but would she marry a man she hardly knew just to keep it in the family? She doubted it.

"Is Jameson still hoping to buy Meredith's portion of the Palmer Ranch?" Laney asked.

Brooke's sister, Meredith, who was estranged from the family and already married, owned the other half of the Palmer Ranch. Laney knew that Jameson wanted to purchase all of Meredith's acreage in order to prevent Samara Lionne, one of Hollywood's biggest movie stars, from buying it for herself.

Brooke nodded. "Yes, but he hasn't had much luck yet. He's really worried that Samara will one day own the entire town of Granger, and to tell you the truth, so am I."

"My father has voiced the same concern," Laney said. "He's still hurt that Wes sold all of his land to her. Plus, there's been no word on what she plans to do with it, so it's a huge mystery. Not to mention the fact that no one knows what Wes is planning on doing with his life, now that he's decided to stop being a rancher."

Wes, Laney's older brother, who was once dubbed one of Montana's Most Eligible Ranchers, seemed to have his sights set on living and earning a living anywhere but Granger. He and his new fiancée, Lydia, who was Samara's former assistant, had spent the past few weeks traveling in Europe. Their next move and the overall drama that had plagued the town for the past several months were the subject of many spirited conversations around the Broward family dinner table.

Laney and Brooke sauntered out of the barn to the fence, taking their time to enjoy the feel of the spring breeze against their skin. They were both country girls at heart. There was no need to rush. Not when everything around them was so beautiful and peaceful.

"I don't think Jameson will ever truly forgive Wes for selling off his portion of the Broward land to Samara," Brooke noted. "I'm sure my sister will sell Samara her half of the Palmer Ranch eventually."

Laney turned toward her. "Why would Meredith do that?"

Brooke leaned against the fence and snorted. "Why wouldn't she? She hasn't set foot in Granger in ages! Plus, Jameson found out that Samara is offering way over market value for the land. My sister has never been one to turn down lots of cold hard cash."

Laney sighed. "Wes can be the same way. Hopefully, married life will soften him and help him rearrange his priorities. I love my brothers and I can't stand when they disagree. I know their little feud keeps my mom up at night. And my dad, he just retreats into his office in the barn."

It hurt Laney's heart to fathom the stress she was about to unleash on her mother and father. They were older now, and although they were still incredibly active, Laney worried about how everything that was going on in their lives was affecting their health. If anything happened to her parents, she didn't know what she would do!

Brooke cleared her throat, interrupting Laney's mental stewing.

"Jameson did tell me that you hired a private investigator, but he wouldn't tell me why. Care to spill the beans?"

Laney glanced away and took in a deep breath of air, which normally would clear her mind, but now it only made her thoughts more muddy.

How could you, Jameson? she thought. She should have known better than to trust her brother with a secret. He was so damn honorable sometimes.

She turned back to Brooke. "He wouldn't tell you why because he doesn't know the reason. It's my business," she stated, struggling to keep her voice even. She didn't want to offend Brooke, but she had to ask the question.

"As is my baby. Please tell me you didn't tell Jameson my secret," she implored.

"No! I didn't tell him anything," said Brooke in a shocked voice. "But after all that he and I went through to be together, we've had enough secrets to last us a lifetime. And we really don't need any more."

Laney bit her lower lip. "I know. I'm sorry to have put you in such an awkward position. I don't want anything to come between you and Jameson. You guys are perfect for each other."

Brooke crossed her arms. "Believe me, I can understand why you want to keep this all a secret. But when are you going to tell your family, Laney? And more important, when are you going to tell him?"

Him.

Austin. The man who was no more than a family friend was now more intertwined with the Browards than anyone realized.

Laney leaned over the railing. "Today. At the family meeting. Everyone will be there and you're right. It's time."

She stared down at her riding boots, caked with mud. Just thinking about telling her parents and her brothers that she was pregnant made her want to saddle up Stella Rose and ride off into the sunset.

Unfortunately, she wasn't sure that this time there would be a happy ending.

Chapter 2

By the time Laney arrived at the BWB Ranch that afternoon, she felt like she was experiencing morning sickness all over again. It was more than just a queasy stomach. There was the sense that something profound was going to happen and there was nothing she could do to stop it.

With one hand on her stomach and the other on the steering wheel, she eased her truck down the winding driveway. She drove as slow as her grandfather, who preferred the other kind of horsepower, and just as cautiously.

The Browards' opulent lodge-style estate often attracted tourists, and out of habit, she ducked her head down a little to avoid being seen. However, today there was no one ogling, no one asking for autographs and no pushy photographers. For once, she wished there were so she could turn around and drive back home.

She pulled her truck around back, joining the other vehicles that were already there. Chokecherry bushes, neatly groomed, lined the private redbrick walkway to the garden entrance of the estate.

She got out and inhaled the sweet scent of lily of the valley, already blooming due to the pervasive rains that had assaulted Granger off and on for the past few weeks. Their delicate white petals were a cheery contrast to the still overcast skies.

She bit her lip and opened the door, but no one was there. Many of the more informal family gatherings were held around the enormous pine table in the kitchen. This meeting must be more serious, she thought, as she hurried through the dining room and to the Great Room.

When she arrived, everyone was seated, but no one was talking and no one looked happy.

Resisting the urge to put her hand on her stomach, she forced herself to walk down the two steps into what, on any other day, was her favorite room in the house. Now it felt like she was stepping into a ticking time bomb.

She popped a smile onto her face. "Why are we meeting in here today and not the kitchen?"

No one answered.

"Okay. Let me guess. Did Dad threaten to cook again?"

Sunlight streamed through the floor-to-ceiling windows, making the room seem too bright. It was so quiet that she could hear the birds chirping outside.

Her stomach tightened again. "What's wrong with everybody?"

Wes and Jameson looked at each other and snickered a little. Although Laney was glad to see that that they seemed to have put their disagreements aside, she had hoped it wouldn't be in solidarity against her.

Gwendolyn, her mother, sat stone-faced in her favorite chair, and seemed to be waiting for something.

Her father strode up to Laney and thrust a newspaper in her face.

"This is what's wrong," he snapped. "Take a good look."

LANEY BROWARD'S BABY BUMP?

Surely that can't be me? Laney thought, her throat constricting in panic.

But there was no mistaking the headline plastered all over the front page of the *Granger Daily News*. It was as clear as the natural springs that dotted the Broward homestead, and as noxious as cow patties.

Even though she had her sunglasses on, the photo in the newspaper was also a dead giveaway. Her signature long hair, cowboy boots and the soon to be not-so-skinny jeans were her standard wardrobe.

Laney took a belated step back in shock. She'd been so careful, but obviously something had gone wrong.

She took hold of the newspaper and her heart thumped in her chest as she read the article.

Laney Broward, one of Granger's most celebrated citizens and the daughter of Steven and Gwendolyn Broward, two of the wealthiest people in the state, was recently spotted in Bozeman, emerging from the office of Dr. Martin McCreedy, a prominent obstetrician who is known for treating Montana's richest women.

Sources close to Ms. Broward, who is a successful horse breeder, reveal that she is currently studying for a master's degree in animal science at Bozeman University. But we have to wonder... is she also enrolled in Parenting 101?

Despite the blaring headline, Laney opened her mouth in protest. But before she could say a word, her father grabbed the paper out of her hands.

"Don't worry. I've already called our attorneys," he sputtered, crumpling the evidence of her indiscretion in one large hand. "We'll slap a libel suit on them quicker than the Granger Parks & Recreation Department can build a stop light!"

Wes sat up on the couch. "Hey, Dad, don't tear up that paper. I want to scan it and post it to Laney's Wikipedia page."

Jameson took out his phone. "And I'll take a picture of it and post it on Facebook. Maybe it will go viral!"

Her brothers high-fived and began to laugh hysterically.

Laney moved past her father and glared at her older brothers. They'd had a habit of picking on her when they were younger, and they still hadn't grown out of it. She'd never been one to fight, but right now they were both asking for it. If only she wasn't pregnant and if only her mother hadn't taught her that ladies never raise their hands—except in class or in prayer.

She clenched her fists. "It's not funny!"

Her grandfather, Charles Broward, the heart and soul of the family, shuffled into the room. He wore his trademark plaid flannel shirt and well-worn blue jeans, except he called them "dungarees," and a deep scowl.

"What's all the commotion about?" he roared, scratching at his chin. "You boys sound like two drunk roosters crowing at dawn."

"Wiki-what?" Steven asked, knitting his brows in confusion.

Both of his sons roared even harder in amusement

at their grandfather's witticisms and their father's lack of internet knowledge.

Steven whistled through his teeth. "Listen, Wes. I know you just got back from God-knows-where and, Jameson, you're still high on life from your honeymoon, but, boys, this is no time for jokes. Right, Laney?"

She turned toward Gwendolyn, who was still sitting silently, a grim look on her face. Their eyes met and Laney saw that not only did her mother sense what was going on, she was very disappointed.

Laney's heart sank, her anger at her brothers chased away by her mother's disapproval.

"You're right. This isn't the time for jokes," she replied quietly, never taking her eyes away from Gwen. "Especially when there's a child at stake."

Her mother covered her hand with her mouth and looked like she was about to cry.

Steven slammed his fist on a small table behind the sofa and tried to smooth out the wrinkles in the newspaper, as if by doing so he could erase the words that could destroy everything he, his father and his great-grandfather, Silas Broward, had built over the past one hundred years.

Jameson slipped his phone back into his pocket. He and Wes looked at each other guiltily, and then at their mother, who continued to frown and say nothing. Grandpa Charles whistled low and slumped against the wall.

And the only sound in the room was the gentle whir of the ceiling fans ten feet above their heads, as her father tried to change what could never be undone.

"I can explain," Laney said quietly. She stared down at the polished wood floors, barely breathing.

Her father looked up from the wrinkled newspaper. "You better," he replied through gritted teeth. His brows knit together and Laney could see that he was struggling not to shout. "Because we all deserve to know."

"Go ahead, honey," her mother urged, her voice remarkably steady. "We're all listening."

Laney took a deep breath and willed herself not to cry. She had to stay strong for herself and her baby.

"What the paper says is true. I'm pregnant."

"Oh, my Lord," Gwendoyln uttered. Her eyes slid shut at the pain she heard in her daughter's voice.

Steven crumpled up the paper again, this time using both fists.

"Well. I'll. Be. Damned."

Wes elbowed Jameson. "So little miss perfect finally got herself knocked up."

"Yeah," Jameson snorted. "The only question I have is, who's the baby daddy?"

Laney whipped around on her heels and stared at her brothers in disbelief at their reaction to her uncomfortable announcement. Gwendolyn clapped her hands, the sound so loud it echoed in the high-ceilinged room.

"Boys! I'm ashamed of you." She spoke sharply, but somehow managed not to raise her voice. "I know this news is a huge shock to all of us, but this is my house and we're still going to talk to each other and treat each other with respect."

"Well said," Grandpa Charles asserted with a stern glare at his grandsons.

Her brothers hung their heads in shame. "Sorry, Mama," each muttered, one after the other.

Laney knew that deep down, Wes and Jameson loved her. They just never realized how much their teasing could hurt, and she knew that they probably never would.

Steven dumped the paper into a nearby trash can. "Well, Laney, should I call the lawyers and have them switch from pursuing a libel suit to chasing a paternity suit? Or are you going to tell us who the father is?"

Laney froze. She knew that her parents had the right to know that Austin was the father of her baby. She even pursed her lips, but was unable to gather the strength to form his name. She knew it was silly, but uttering Austin's name aloud to her family would somehow make the one night they'd spent together feel cheap. When in reality their lovemaking was anything but meaningless, at least to Laney.

Gwendolyn stood and walked over to her daughter.

"Let Laney speak. You're not giving her a chance to tell us what's going on."

She held out her hand and Laney took it, feeling like a little girl, wanting and needing her mother's love. They walked over to the sofa and sat down.

"Now, how far along are you?"

Laney slipped her hand away, suddenly ashamed.

"Four months. The picture in the newspaper must have been taken after my last appointment with Dr. McCreedy."

"Why didn't you tell us?" Gwen put her arm around her shoulders, and Laney felt like crying again.

"I wanted to, Mom. I really did," she choked out, struggling to keep her emotions encased in her heart.

"But with Wes and Lydia's engagement, and then Jameson and Brooke's wedding, plus everything else going on, it never seemed like the right time."

She looked into her mother's eyes, pleading with her

to understand. "I'm sorry you had to find out like this. I'm sorry that I brought all this trouble and—"

Her words were cut off by the sound of the doorbell and everything stopped. Except the guilt. It reverberated throughout Laney's body, like a harsh, recurring chime, an ache of warning.

"Are you expecting anyone, Gwendolyn?" Steven asked.

"No, I'm not."

He turned to Wes. "Get the door," he ordered. "Whoever it is, get rid of them. We still have a lot to discuss here."

No one spoke, but if they had, it wouldn't have broken the thick net of tension in the room. When Wes returned a minute or so later, all eyes were on their guest: Austin Johns.

What was he doing in Granger?

"Look what the tumbleweed rolled in," joked Wes, glad to have a break from his sister's latest drama.

Laney's mouth parted at the sight of him. He wore neatly pressed khakis, a light blue button-down shirt and a very unfriendly frown.

Her eyes traced his lips and she distinctly remembered how they felt upon her skin, erupting the same passion that stirred within her now.

Laney noticed right away that he avoided looking at her, even though where she was sitting with her mother was directly opposite him. In fact, he seemed to be looking right through her.

I might as well be invisible, she thought.

In a way, it was good, and she quickly tried to think of a plan to escape this uncomfortable scene without arousing suspicion.

Laney straightened her body ever-so-slightly, so that her mother would not notice, even though inside, she wished she could flatten herself like a cartoon character and slide beneath the seat cushions.

Gwendolyn rose and went to greet him. "Austin! What a pleasant surprise."

Austin swept his Stetson from his head and bowed. "Hello, Mrs. Broward."

He turned and stuck out his hand. "Mr. Broward. I'm so sorry to disturb you on a Sunday afternoon, sir."

"Austin," Steven said, returning the gesture brusquely. His eyes slanted distractedly toward the trash container and then back again. "What can we do for you?"

"Are you here to discuss your horses?" Gwendolyn asked. "I hear you purchased a new foal. I'd love to hear more."

Austin smiled, but it didn't reach his eyes. "I have, and he's a beautiful animal. As much as I'd like to, I'm not here to talk about my recent acquisitions."

He turned toward Laney and her heart beat faster, yet his dark eyes regarded her with muted interest, as if she were no more than a mannequin in a department store window.

"Instead I was wondering if I might have a private word with Laney."

Even though his eyes were on her, the question seemed as though it was addressed to her parents, as if she were a child.

Laney felt her stomach burn at Austin's arrogance. Didn't she have any say in the matter?

Anxiety sluiced through her insides. What could he possibly want to talk about?

She hadn't seen him since New Year's Eve. Though she'd dreamed about him frequently, she wasn't sure she wanted to see the father of her baby, or be alone with him.

He deserves to know.

Laney pushed the thought to the back of her mind. Not now. Not here!

Steven crossed his arms and twisted his chin toward his wife. Gwendolyn shrugged, as baffled as her husband.

Austin was businesslike and professional, just as he normally was, yet the tone of his voice and his polite yet distant manner seemed imbued with deeper purpose.

They could count on two fingers the times when Austin had been at the Granger homestead and had not wanted to talk about horses. Both were after he had suffered some unfortunate losses in his stables. He'd come to Gwendolyn and Steven, fellow ranchers and horse breeders, not so much for advice, but for comfort.

This third time was different and they both knew it, but they had no idea why.

After an awkward pause, Gwendolyn spoke first. "Well, if it's okay with Laney…"

"It's fine, Mama," Laney told her mother firmly, even though it wasn't.

She stood, her knees wobbling a bit. The spring minidress she wore wasn't form-fitting. It had tiny pink roses on a black background that hid any pudginess around her middle. But she still had to resist the urge to run her hand across her abdomen to check if she was showing.

Her father sat down in a wide leather chair. "Make it quick," he grumbled, sounding defeated. "Remember, we're in the middle of a family meeting and we all have a lot more to discuss."

Laney avoided looking at her older brothers, still upset by their teasing. "I'm sure we won't be long," she replied as she walked out of the room.

Only as long as it took to make sure that Austin stayed out of her and her baby's life.

Austin watched Laney's slender frame carefully as she led him to another part of the house. He had to hand it to her—she certainly didn't look pregnant.

Her dress, which fell midthigh, swished across her long, bare legs. He let the memories flow back and he felt himself go hard, remembering their feverish love-making. How her thighs had locked around his torso, as he'd charged like a train roaring through the night, as if she'd wanted him to stay there forever. And he would have, had she not let him go.

Austin was glad Laney couldn't look at his face right now and see how much he still wanted her. Being this close after so many months apart was like seeing a mirage in the desert. Thirsty with a lust he'd tamped down for months, he welcomed the sight of her, despite the fact that he was angry.

Maybe it's not true.

Austin wedged the paper even farther under his arm. That's what he was here to find out, and he wasn't going to let his attraction to her distract him from finding out the truth.

He didn't know if the Browards had seen the head-line yet. When he'd read it that morning, he was so shocked that he nearly choked on his protein shake. He had to talk to Laney before they did. His whole future depended on it.

"Where are we headed?"

Laney tossed her long brown hair over her shoulder. "To the library. It's in another wing of the house. We're almost there."

"No worries," he responded. It gave him more time to enjoy the view, as she moved down the hall with athletic grace.

Hadn't he read somewhere that women got wider when they were carrying a baby? Laney appeared to be the same size and beautiful shape that she'd been on New Year's Eve. Of course, he'd have to feel her to find out and he wouldn't have any problem doing that experiment. Austin wasn't the type to beg. However, if that's what it took to be with Laney again, he just might.

Seconds later, they arrived and he waited while Laney opened the mahogany double doors.

He stepped inside the room. It was wall-to-wall books, but he was willing to bet that none of them contained the secret to winning this woman's heart.

She eased the doors shut, turned and crossed her arms. "What are you doing in Granger?" Her words tumbled out of her mouth, as if she were in a rush. She hadn't even bothered to offer him a seat.

But Austin had all the time in the world.

He took the paper from under his arm and unfolded it. He'd only brought the front page. It was the only section that mattered.

Austin held the newspaper in front of him and watched her stare at it without blinking. And when her brown eyes moved to his face, he ignored the pull of desire.

Then he pointed at her belly. It was time to stop being polite. It was time for answers.

"It's mine, isn't it?"

"You can't possibly believe—"

He strode up to her and held the paper next to his ear. "Just answer the question, Laney."

She turned away from him, refusing to look at it. "You're being ridiculous. How can you believe that trash?"

"It's mine, isn't it," he repeated in a clipped voice. "How far along are you?"

She swiveled around and folded her arms at her chest.

"Wow, Austin. You don't say hi or 'How do you do,'" she said coolly. "You just storm into my life with a question that's out of context and quite frankly, none of your business."

He tossed the paper down on the leather couch. It immediately slid to the floor, the headline mocking them both. Even so, both were prideful and neither of them moved to pick up the newspaper.

His eyes flitted down to her stomach and immediately back up to her face.

"Let me paint a picture for you. New Year's Eve. You and me. In my bed. Banging each other like it was Armageddon outside and we were the last two people on earth. Is that enough context for you?"

Her eyes flickered with subdued rage. "How dare you! Is that all that night was to you? You screwing me like an oversexed frat boy?"

She spun around and his groin tightened as he watched her walk away.

God, no, he wanted to yell. One night with her had changed his whole life, but he knew she wasn't ready to hear that yet, much like he wasn't quite ready to completely believe it himself.

He hadn't touched another woman since, even though he'd had plenty of opportunities. Abstinence wasn't his strong suit and he still wasn't completely used to it. But a man could change, for the right woman, and that's what he was here to find out.

There's still so much I don't know about her.

"Now, I'm going to ask you one more time. Is the baby mine?"

He tightened his jaw and waited. After a few moments, he strode over to where she stood by the window and touched her elbow.

She twisted away roughly, as if her skin were on fire.

"Four months," she hissed.

His mouth dropped open. "Wh-what?"

For once, he was able to push the sensual memories of Laney out of his mind, so he could do the math.

"Four months," she repeated more curtly. "That's the answer to your question."

Austin stared at her, stomach roiling, his mind almost numb with shock. He was glad he'd skipped lunch.

"So it is mine."

His voice sounded garbled in his ears, as if his words were spoken underwater.

Laney tilted her chin up. "Correction," she asserted. "It's mine. This baby doesn't concern you."

If her defiant tone was meant to let him off the hook, it backfired. Instead, it only served to anger him.

He squared his hands on his hips. "What are you talking about, Laney? I'm the father."

Her eyes crept over his body, as if she still couldn't

believe it was true, making him contemplate the gravity of that one word:

Father.

That one word led to a world of diapers and daycare and sleepless nights. It also led to Laney.

Her shoulders slumped in defeat. "This wasn't supposed to happen, okay? I was protected. You were protected."

She stared at him and shook her head, before facing the window and closing her eyes. Austin wondered what was going through her mind. Had she thought about him since?

That night, neither of them was drunk. They were both fully cognizant of what they wanted and what they were doing.

Austin hadn't bothered to ask if she were on birth control, he'd just used a condom as he always did. It was just the right thing to do.

But something must have gone wrong.

He thought back to the utter veracity of their coupling. It was like he'd lost his mind or something and she'd kept urging him to go faster and faster, and plunge deeper and deeper. Willingly he'd complied. All night and far into the morning until she'd said goodbye and he'd never heard from her again.

He swallowed hard as his desire for her once again swept through him. How he longed to place his hands on her bare legs, lift her dress and—

Austin cleared his throat and forced himself to concentrate. "It wasn't supposed to happen, but it did. The question now is—what are we going to do about it?"

She glanced back over her shoulder. "*We* aren't going

to do anything. I'm not holding you to any obligation here. It happened. Let's just leave it at that, okay?"

He arched a brow at Laney's tone, hardly believing that she could be so casual about this situation. His question was a sensible one. Not only that, unlike the college frat boy that she obviously thought he was, it was responsible.

He stared at her. "Does your family know?"

She turned and nodded. "That's what we were discussing when you came in."

He took a deep breath. That's what he'd been afraid of.

Steven and Gwendolyn Broward were powerful influencers in the Granger community and he'd heard that nothing worthwhile happened in town without their complete buy-in.

Steven had even emailed him some articles about a new influx of wannabe ranchers that could threaten their stronghold. However, even as an outsider looking in, based on his past dealings with them, he was confident that the Browards would prevail. He also had no doubt that the wealthy couple had the same strong influence on their family.

Suddenly, his heart clenched in his chest and he steeled himself to ask the most difficult question of all.

"You're keeping it, right?"

Her eyes widened in shock. "Of course I am," she cried out, aghast. "How could you even have the gall to ask me that? This baby is mine."

Austin breathed an inward sigh of relief. "I didn't mean to offend you, but you know I had to ask because this baby is my responsibility, too."

A scowl marred her pretty face and he hated to see it. Would he ever be able to make her smile again?

"I don't want anything from you, Austin."

"That's not what I mean and you know it. As the child's father, I have legal rights, not to mention a moral obligation."

Not to mention that I'm still attracted to you.

Still, having been played for a fool before, he had to be cautious. Due to the Broward family wealth, he was confident that Laney was not after his money, and right now, that's all he had to give her.

His heart was off-limits.

He moved toward Laney, wanting to embrace her, unsure if she would accept him. He wasn't about to go chasing after a woman who wasn't interested in him. That is, unless that woman was carrying his child.

"Moral obligation aside," Laney insisted, her voice tight. "It's not like I can't afford a baby. We'll be fine."

"That may be so," he said, moving closer. "But I still want to help."

Suddenly she whirled away, out of his reach, taking his gentle feelings with it.

"Stay away from me, Austin," she warned, her brown eyes flashing dangerously. "Stay away from me. And my baby."

So that's the way she's going to play this.

Austin clenched his jaw so tight that his head started to ache. He didn't understand why Laney was so offended by him, by his willingness to be a part of the child's life. He didn't want things to be this way, but he had no choice.

"Fine. First thing tomorrow, I'm going to get in touch with my lawyers," he informed her in a smooth voice.

"There are legal papers that must be drawn up immediately."

Laney dropped her hands to the side and by her glare he could see that his words bothered her.

"And we'll need to look into DNA testing to prove I'm the father," he added quickly.

Laney put her hands on her hips. The look on her face could have quelled a tornado. "I haven't been with anyone since that night," she insisted. "You're either trying to insinuate that I sleep around or you don't believe me. Which is it?"

"Neither," he assured her, hiding a smile. Although he was sorry he'd upset her, he was pleased to hear that no other man had touched her.

"I'm just trying to make sure that I follow the proper processes for joint custody," he replied blithely. "And of course, I will incorporate the child into my will. It's the right thing to do financially."

Austin's family owned an expansive ranch outside of Dallas. Although his father was a high-powered executive in the oil industry, Austin had no desire to follow in his dad's footsteps. Instead, he developed an interest in horses as a child. He began breeding thoroughbreds in his twenties, while dabbling in the stock market at the same time. Luckily, he'd been successful in both ventures.

With his wealth and Laney's combined, their child would never have to worry about money.

Laney narrowed her eyes at him. "What kind of father could you possibly be, Austin? Traveling all the time from one city to one country to the next? How could you be here for the child?"

Austin wondered the same thing, but she didn't have

to know. Letting her know that at this moment he felt completely unprepared and unqualified to be a father would only make things worse for him.

He swallowed down the doubt that threatened to flood his senses. "You just stay healthy and let me worry about the logistics," he said sternly.

Laney shook her head. "I won't let you do this, Austin," she vowed. "It will never work."

"What is it that won't work?" he demanded.

She didn't answer. Instead, she walked away and stood near the fireplace. What had happened to the warm and loving woman he'd kissed on New Year's Eve? Now she seemed cold and unfeeling.

He strode over to her and put his hands on her shoulders, gently forcing her to look at him.

"Why are you being so stubborn?"

She shrugged away from his grasp. "And why are you trying to infringe on my life?" she replied hotly.

"It's not like I'm asking to marry you," he shot back.

Her face crumpled a bit and his heart twinged in his chest, knowing that somehow his comment hurt her, but having no idea why it would.

She walked away silently and he opened his mouth to apologize, but he knew it wouldn't do any good.

Laney stood in front of the bay window, her back ramrod-straight. Through the large panes, he could see waves of prairie grass where many of the Browards' prized heritage cattle grazed, blissfully unaware of anything but filling their bellies.

"I wouldn't marry you anyway, Austin," she said quietly, not facing him. "You and I are far too different. Other than our love of land and horses, we have nothing in common."

Though he knew he deserved it, her words still tore at his heart. If he had a touch less pride, he might have suggested a marriage of convenience, but there was no way he would ever marry a woman he didn't love.

It was clear that Laney wanted nothing more to do with him. Even though she'd admitted that she hadn't shared her bed with anyone else since that night, that didn't mean she wanted to share it with him again.

Austin joined Laney at the window, keeping a respectable distance, even though he wanted to reach out and draw her to him.

He turned his face toward hers, wondering how he would be able to hide his desire for her, both physically and emotionally.

"That's not true anymore, Laney. We have our baby."

She thinned her lips and refused to look at him. "I can't talk about all this now. Can you just go? Just leave!"

Austin deftly squeezed into a space between Laney and the window. He tilted her chin up, forcing her to look at him.

"Let me make this clear," he said quickly, before she even thought of getting away. "That night? I didn't want it to end. I tried to get in touch with you, but you wouldn't return my calls."

She opened her mouth to speak, and he put his finger against her lips. Whatever she had to say didn't matter anymore.

"Let me finish. If you think you're going to play the same game with my child, you better think again. I'm not the man you think I am and I won't be played for a fool."

Without another word, Austin stalked out of the room

and down the hallway, knowing that Laney wouldn't bother to run after him.

When he reached the Great Room, none of the Browards were there. In fact, the entire place seemed to be deserted and he wasn't in the mood to go looking for someone to thank them for their hospitality.

He stalked to his truck, got in and slammed the door. His tires squealed as he peeled away. He waited until he was off the Broward property before he stopped and picked up his cell phone.

"Fifty," he muttered.

The call picked up in seconds.

"Austin. Long time no hear from."

The voice on the other end had that cheerful, Midwestern twang that always set his nerves on edge, especially when he was pissed off.

"Hey, Morty. How's things?"

"They're predicting another huge windstorm in Chicago. My hair can't take it."

Austin rolled his eyes. The man was as bald as a cue ball, but with no luck.

"You don't have any hair, Mort."

"Yeah. The damn wind blew it all away!"

Austin laughed, in spite of his sour mood.

"What can I do for you, my friend?" Morty asked pleasantly.

"I need a place to stay," Austin responded, idly watching a beat-up truck hauling a trailer full of sheep down the opposite side of the road.

"Where are you off to now? Rome? Istanbul? Antarctica? I got a line on an igloo that actually floats on a glacier."

Morty Greer was an old-school travel agent, a licensed real estate broker and a gambling addict. His poison: horse racing.

Austin had met him after his prized thoroughbred, The Perfect Shot, had won Morty a ton of money. They'd even had their picture taken together. Austin began to let Morty handle all of his travel arrangements and eventually the two men became friends.

Over time, Morty's travel agency took a serious hit care of name-your-own-price websites and smartphone ticketing.

Then Morty's money started dwindling away, or rather, he'd gambled it away. Austin felt sorry for his friend, so he made him a deal: get treatment for gambling and Austin would find something that would keep him busy and employed.

The arrangement had worked out for both of them.

Morty had been clean for over a year, and Austin had a personal concierge.

"I'm not keen on freezing my ass off, Mort."

"Smart man!"

Austin chuckled and continued, "Remember that little town in Montana called Granger? I've got a few clients here."

"Yeah, I remember. You usually do an in-and-out through Bozeman. What time do you need to arrive?"

Austin could hear Morty typing on his keyboard.

"Actually, I'm already here. And this time, I'm staying."

The tapping stopped. "How long?"

But before Austin could say anything, Morty started typing and talking.

"Let me see if I can find you a nice hotel. There's one right in town called The Granger Inn." Morty paused, and then swore. "But it's booked solid for the next few months."

"I think I'm going to be here awhile, Mort. Are there any rental properties available? You know my standards."

Morty grunted. "Yeah, I do. They're about as high as the Sears Tower and just as expensive. But with a few clicks of the mouse… Got it. There's a few homes that are for rent and currently unoccupied. How long of a lease do you need?"

Austin thought a moment. He really had no idea.

How long would it take to complete the DNA testing, get the custody papers completed and signed and convince Laney that she was wrong about him?

The baby was due in September.

His baby.

And he wasn't going to allow Laney or anyone else to keep him away from his child.

"Six months. I'll let you know if I need it for longer. I'd like to look at some this evening, if possible."

"You got it. I'll make some calls and email you a list of properties as soon as I've vetted them."

"Thanks, Morty."

"What are you doing in Montana anyway? Trying to catch a cowgirl?"

"Nope, just trying to take down a bull."

Morty snorted. "Aren't we all?"

Austin laughed as he tossed his phone on the seat and started down the road.

A beautiful, headstrong woman like Laney could never be caught. She was too busy running. And at this point, it looked like she had the upper hand and had gained some considerable distance.

Despite breeding thoroughbred racehorses, Austin wasn't a gambling man with his heart. Still he was willing to bet that Laney's early advantage wouldn't last.

Chapter 3

Laney pressed her palm against the window and watched Austin's black truck peel away, so fast that if the ground wasn't wet from all the rain, it would have kicked up a dust storm.

She'd never seen Austin angry. The only emotion she'd ever seen in him was desire. Now he probably hated her for driving him away. Again.

Gingerly, she dropped onto the comfy window seat and leaned against the pillows.

How she'd missed him!

She closed her eyes, relishing in the familiar, sweet tug in her abdomen that occurred whenever she thought about how good he'd made her feel that night.

There had been no indication on his part that their "relationship" would last any longer than a few hours. There were no promises made. No secrets told. Nothing but raw, unadulterated sex.

Austin had called her a few times. That much was true. But she'd figured he was only making an obligatory gesture, so she wouldn't think he was a tool, and she a mere toy.

Then why had she been thinking about him for the past four months?

Because you're carrying his child.

She ran her hands over her belly, trying to feel the life that was growing inside her.

That was all it was. The baby was their only connection. There was nothing else, and yet something about Austin wanting to be so involved with her life, and so quickly, got her back up. Made her slightly uncomfortable. She wasn't having it. No way. She didn't need anyone to take care of her—or her baby.

She could do this on her own.

Hopefully, he'd gotten the message.

Her head felt like it was spinning as she tried to take in all that had transpired.

She knew Austin had legal rights and a moral obligation, but there had to be more than that. Why would someone like Austin want to be tied down with a baby? The man was too busy to have a relationship, let alone to raise a child. He just didn't realize it yet.

Laney shivered. All that talk about legal contracts, a DNA test, joint custody and, God forbid, a will. Yes, she had one, but just thinking about her eventual demise gave her the creeps.

Was Austin merely so shocked by the prospect of being a father that he was moved to instant action, or were his words simply a threat?

Laney drew her knees up to her chest. Or were they, like his phone calls, merely obligatory? A means to save his reputation and perhaps his business relationship with the Browards?

Since Laney didn't really know Austin, she couldn't say whether or not he would follow through on anything.

But she did know that money was a motivator. He loved to make it and he loved to spend it, and he loved to be around people who could help him make even more. Namely, the Browards.

Austin never had said why he was in Granger in the first place. *Maybe he's going to try to buy up some of the town like that awful Samara Lionne,* Laney thought.

The A-list actress even had the nerve to throw her own gala to welcome her to town. Pretty soon, she'd probably carve her own star onto Main Street.

Laney shook her head. Although the event was still a few weeks away, she shuddered to think about what she would wear, and the reaction she would get from everyone when she walked in alone—and pregnant.

She closed her eyes and all she saw was Austin's gorgeous face. Getting rid of him was the right thing to do.

After all, Austin was from Texas. And as far as she was concerned, Montana was a world away from the Lone Star State.

Like Samara, Austin was an outsider and couldn't be trusted.

When she felt she was up to it, Laney snuck into the powder room and splashed cold water on her face. She looked in the mirror as she patted her cheeks with a towel.

The truth was out, but she felt no relief. Only fear. Her family still didn't know who the father of her baby was, and she didn't know how she was going to tell them it was Austin.

She ambled down the long hallway to the other wing. The Great Room was empty, but there was a wonderful odor in the air: her mother's signature peanut-butter cookies.

The Browards had their own chef six days a week.

The only time Gwendolyn turned on the stove was on Sundays and during a crisis.

Laney hesitated just outside the kitchen door.

She had always been independent. It was her mother who had encouraged her love for horses, to start riding for fun and then for sport. Gwen had always been there to pick her up when she fell and to cheer her on.

How disappointed she must be in me now!

She walked into the kitchen, avoiding everyone's eyes but those of her mother.

"How many batches are you making this time?" she asked timidly.

Gwen pushed herself away from the counter. "Only two," she responded, her lips breaking into a smile. "One batch for you and one for the baby."

Tears sprang to Laney's eyes at her mother's kindness and understanding.

"That's if Wes and I don't eat them all first," Jameson said glibly.

But Laney barely heard him. Her eyes were still focused on Gwen.

"Mom…I'm so sorry!"

The tears fell freely now as she collapsed into her mother's open arms.

"Shh… This child is not a mistake. He or she is a blessing."

Wes looked down at the worn pine table, uncomfortable at the scene before him. Up until now, his sister had never done anything even remotely stupid. He didn't know what to say to her. All he knew was that his family didn't need any more scandal their lives.

Jameson stretched his long legs out and frowned as

he observed Laney sobbing. He was starting to worry about her.

A few weeks back, when Laney had asked him for the name of a private investigator, he'd given her one with no questions asked. She'd assured him that she was not in danger.

Perhaps now, with a baby on the way, it was time for him to get some answers. If something happened to Laney, he would never forgive himself.

Steven shoved his hands in his pockets and looked away. He hated to see anyone cry, especially his only daughter. Then he remembered Austin and clenched his fists. Was he the cause of all her tears?

The oven timer dinged and everyone jumped. Laney released her grip on her mom so she could tend to the cookies.

"Sit down, honey. You look exhausted."

Laney pulled out a chair, and slowly eased herself into it. She was tired. Whether it was from being pregnant, from stress or from the excitement of seeing Austin after all those months, she didn't know, but she knew that if she would lay her head down on the table it would be lights out.

Gwen gave her a strange look and then pointed her spatula at her younger son.

"Jameson, go grab Laney a pillow from the sofa in the Great Room so she can rest her back against it," she ordered. "Wes. I've got a pitcher of milk in the refrigerator. Get it out and put it on the table, please."

Gwen slipped on her oven mitts like a prizefighter getting ready to step into the ring.

"And, Steven, wipe that hangdog look off your face. This is supposed to be a happy occasion."

"I agree. Cheer up, son," Grandpa Charles admonished. "This is no different than birthing a calf."

Steven shot his father a look. "The hell it isn't, Dad. This is my daughter we're talking about."

And she wasn't going to get off that easy.

Gwendolyn could coddle her if she wanted, like she always did, but somebody had to restore order and discipline in the Broward household, and that someone was him.

Never mind the fact that all of his children were grown and living on their own. In fact, they each had their own homes on Broward property.

Wes and Jameson worked on the ranch. Although lately, Wes was around much less often than Steven would have preferred, he thought with a grimace. Now that Wes was engaged to Lydia, they traveled a lot. Steven hoped that they'd soon settle down, get married and start a family.

Unfortunately, he had no idea when that would happen or where Wes would end up living permanently. His mind still simmered in anger at his son who had recently sold his homestead without discussing it with the family to Samara Lionne, some actress he'd never even heard of until she'd suddenly decided that Granger would be the perfect place to buy a second home.

Jameson was his loyal one. He loved the land, the BWB Heritage Ranch and the great state of Montana as much as he did. His new wife, Brooke, had ranching in her blood, although Steven was quickly learning that she'd rather play with clay than herd cattle. He prayed that Brooke wouldn't lead his younger son away from his true purpose in life: running the Broward family ranch.

Twenty years ago, when Steven had taken over the

day-to-day running of the ranch from his father, some folks in Granger had gossiped that he'd run it right into the ground. His notions about cattle breeding seemed downright insane to his more conservative neighbors. His innovative idea to specialize in breeding high-end cattle and heritage farm animals ended up putting the Broward family name on the map. The Browards went from being well-off to being filthy rich.

Laney had her horse breeding business and it was very successful. Even though the gold medal that she never wanted to show off had attracted a lot of gawkers, rancher wannabes and other crazy folk to Granger, he was proud of her accomplishments.

Like her mother, she'd always been independent, ambitious and sometimes a pain in the ass. Though he'd never pegged his daughter as a wild child, something must have happened to change her.

Steven took his hands out of his pockets and turned to Laney. "How could you let a thing like this happen?" he demanded. "For God's sake, you're not even married!"

At his harsh words, Laney stopped sobbing and a hush fell over the room.

"I'm sorry, Dad. I can explain," she pleaded, her face stained with tears.

Jameson walked into the room and handed Laney a small round pillow. "Thank you," she said gratefully. She wedged it behind her back and sighed in relief.

He slid into his chair and glanced at the silent faces of his normally boisterous family.

"What did I miss?" he asked.

"Hush, Jameson. Let Laney talk," Gwen instructed.

She put a platter of warm cookies in the middle of the table. No one moved to take one.

Laney took one whiff and immediately felt nauseated. Normally, she'd start to gobble them up. But right now she could barely look at them, let alone eat them, but she didn't have the heart to ask her mother to take them away.

She bit her lip and began. "Remember the gala I attended on New Year's Eve?"

Steven looked confused, but Gwen remembered right away.

"It was in Dallas, right? You were getting together with your friends Maya and Robyn."

Laney nodded. "I hadn't seen them in such a long time. Anyway, Austin was there. He was one of the event sponsors and, well, uh—"

She paused, stifling the urge to squirm in her seat.

How could she tell the story without making herself sound cheap? She didn't want to talk about his kiss. She didn't want to even say his name again.

"Just spill it, Laney," Jameson urged, hoping she would provide some clue as to why she had hired a private detective.

Laney slanted her eyes at her brother and steeled her voice once more.

"Austin came up to me and we talked. And one thing led to another and—"

Bam! Wes set the pitcher of milk down hard on the table and everyone jumped. He sat down. "Spare us the gory details, Laney."

"That must have been some talk," Jameson said, half-jokingly.

No one else said a word.

"Is Austin the father of your baby?" her mother asked quietly.

Laney paused only a moment before nodding. She felt an immediate sense of relief, but the feeling was quickly replaced by shame as her father's voice exploded into the taut silence.

"But you barely know him! Didn't you use birth control?"

Laney's cheeks burned. Talking about sex was difficult enough with anyone. But talking about it with her entire family was something akin to torture.

"We did but it must have failed," she insisted, trying desperately to defend herself. "That does happen, you know."

Wes and Jameson glanced at one another, as if they had some personal experience, and then just as quickly avoided each other's eyes.

Steven snorted. "So that was the reason for Austin's unannounced visit. He saw the headlines, did the math and—"

"Hellooo, Daddy," muttered Grandpa Charles. "Well, at least he's not after the Broward fortune. He's got his own."

Gwen shot both men a look. "Austin Johns is a good man. I've dealt with him plenty of times. He's honest, forthright and—"

"A Texan." Steven finished. There was no use arguing with Gwen when she liked someone. "You can tell him we don't have any oil on our land. Just cows and horses."

"Steven, really!" Gwen said in an exasperated voice. "He's not interested in our land."

"Hrmph. Maybe not, but I wouldn't put it past him. What did he say when you told him he was the father?"

"He said he wanted to help."

"Well…well…well." Her father reached for a cookie. "I think he's helped enough."

Laney stared at her father, on the verge of tears again. How could he be so unfeeling?

"Dad, I don't know how many times I can apologize, but I'm sorry I disappointed you all."

Her mother put her hands on Laney's shoulders and squeezed.

"Honey, a baby is never a disappointment. This is certainly a surprise, but it's also wonderful news. You're going to have the first Broward heir!"

Laney turned her head and kissed one of Gwen's hands. "Thanks, Mom."

"Boys?"

Wes was the first to offer his congratulations.

"I ought to thank you for letting me off the hook," he said as he leaned down and gave her a hug. "Lydia hasn't talked about having babies yet, but I'm kinda glad we won't be the first. We have a lot of plans!"

Jameson arched a brow. "Care to reveal any of them?"

"Not yet. We're still firming up the details, but I'll share the news as soon as I can."

Grandpa Charles coughed. "Laney, I still don't understand how you managed to hide things. You still look as slender as a whip. Same as the day you graduated from high school."

Gwen took a closer look at her daughter. "I agree. I remember when I was pregnant with Wes, I had a little baby bump at three months. Wes was a big boy."

"With a big mouth," Grandpa interjected.

Laney laughed. "I'm not that thin. I just eat well and choose my wardrobe wisely."

Grandpa chuckled and patted his ample stomach.

"Two things I don't do. Maybe I can learn something from you." He reached for his third cookie. "Then again, maybe not!"

Jameson got up and gave his sister a reluctant hug, unsure of how to act around her now.

"Congratulations. Now that your secret is out, does this mean you won't need the private investigator anymore? Because if not, I'd like to get him on Wes's case. If he won't tell us what he's got planned, that guy will."

Jameson didn't want to ask the question, but he figured that was the only way he'd get a straight answer from her.

Gwen dropped her hands from Laney's shoulders and pulled out the chair next to her. "Private investigator? What's going on?"

Laney wanted to scream. First her brother told his wife about the investigator, now he had to spill it to their entire family.

"I hired him because I thought someone was trying to blackmail me."

"Why would you think that?" Gwen asked, a note of fear in her voice.

"A few weeks ago, I got an anonymous email through my school account telling me that if he didn't receive a certain amount of money, he would tell the whole world my secret."

"You actually paid this person?" Wes asked.

Laney nodded. "I guess he didn't like the amount I gave him."

"How much?" her father asked.

"You don't want to know."

Her mother took in a sharp breath. "Did you ever meet him?"

"No. I've never even spoken to him. I wired the money to a special account. I thought everything was taken care of, but I still wanted to try to find out the person's identity. That's when I asked Jameson for the name of a private detective."

"Laney, I don't like this one bit," Gwen said, her voice shaking a bit. "What if he tries to hurt you?"

"How do you know it's a him?" Wes said.

"Actually, I don't know if it was a male or a female," Laney admitted. "The email was signed 'The Cobra.'"

"Sounds like a male to me," Steven said.

"Sounds like a snake," asserted Wes.

"Sounds like you need a bodyguard," Jameson surmised, draping his arm around his sister's shoulders.

"I agree," said her mother.

"I don't. I'm not going to be constrained by a bodyguard or by fear. I'm fine."

"Why would somebody do this? Do you know anybody in Bozeman who would want to hurt you?"

Laney shook her head. "Not really. My classmates seem cool. They're all great people who care about animals, just like me."

Steven sighed. He'd always thought his daughter was a little too trusting. For proof, all he had to do was look at the situation she was in now with Austin.

"You were always as stubborn as those horses you raise. Just be careful," he said roughly.

"I will, Daddy."

He nodded. "I hate to be the one who has to issue a reality check, but I'm concerned about the additional attention that this news will now bring to the family. I was hoping that things would let up a little bit. Get a little quieter around here."

"Truthfully, I was, too," Laney said. "I'm really sorry about this."

Gwen went and hugged her husband. "Will you stop worrying so much? Everything will be okay. You'll see."

Grandpa clapped his hands together. "Enough with the lovey-dovey stuff. Are you having a boy or a girl?"

"I don't know yet," Laney responded, reaching into her purse. "Do you all want to see a picture of the baby?"

She waited until they were all gathered around her before she passed the sonogram around.

The baby was real now. To all of them.

Grandpa scratched his chin. "I think it's a boy—look at those hands! They'll be as old as mine someday," he said, wriggling his fingers.

"Look at those chubby cheeks," Jameson teased. "I think it's a girl."

He passed the sonogram printout to Wes.

"It doesn't look like much," said Wes, passing it to his father.

Steven stared at the image. The sight of the blurred figure made him tear up a little, but he didn't want anyone to know.

"It looks like you," her father coughed and quickly passed the thin sheet of paper to his wife.

"How can you tell?" Laney asked.

"Because it's beautiful," Gwendolyn said, choking back tears. "Oh, Laney, I'm so sorry you didn't feel like you could come to us sooner."

"We're not the problem here, Gwen," Steven grumbled, trying to infuse some parental reality into the warmth of the moment. But one look in his wife's eyes told him that he was wrong.

"Oh, yes, we are. Our daughter didn't feel comfortable talking with us. She felt she had to keep our first grandchild a secret. Don't you think *that's* a problem?"

Grandpa Charles grunted in agreement. "I would say it is. If children, even grown, can't turn to their parents, who can they turn to?"

"We're going to put that all behind us now," Gwen stated emphatically. "Let's make a pact. Between all of us. No More Secrets. The Broward family needs to stay strong and stay together, now more than ever."

Gwen made a fist and put it in the middle of the table. Grandpa was the first to stick out his hand and lay it over hers. Then Jameson and Wes. Laney was next.

"Dad?" Jameson asked. "What about you?"

Laney turned her head and looked up at her father, afraid of what she'd see in his eyes.

In her eyes, Steven saw a deep love for him and their entire family that would nourish and sustain a future generation of Browards. Destroying their bond through unforgiveness would go against everything he'd ever taught his daughter.

"I hope he likes cattle. We can always use some more help around the ranch," he said gruffly.

Holding back tears, Steven reached out his hand and placed it gently over hers.

Chapter 4

Laney stepped out of her mother's red convertible in front of The Sunflower Café, Granger's only upscale eatery, with an even worse sense of dread than she'd felt twelve hours earlier.

Since she'd told Gwen about the baby, her mom had all kinds of decorating ideas for the nursery. The plan was to eat a light breakfast and then head down to Bozeman for some serious shopping.

Although she was looking forward to spending some long-overdue quality time with her mother, she wasn't quite sure she was ready to face the good people of Granger yet.

Since the news broke yesterday, the media backlash had been brutal and her publicist was working desperately to find the "positive spin" in the story. It would only be a matter of time before everyone learned who was responsible for her "baby bump."

And then the real firestorm would begin.

She had to be ready for it. Clearly, the media was no longer her BFF, they were her sworn enemy. Now was the time to protect her already damaged reputation and that of the Broward family.

She'd already placed a call that morning to the private

investigator she'd hired in the hopes that he'd be able to find out who was responsible for leaking the story. Was it The Cobra, the person who'd blackmailed her? Or someone else?

Laney wasn't about to sit back and wait for an answer.

She had her own agenda. Her plan was to find out as much information about Austin as she could.

Discreetly, of course.

Her mother had eyes in the back of her head and ears that homed in like radar. Laney knew she was probably having a hard time coming to grips with the fact that she didn't know her own daughter was pregnant. Avoiding the BWB ranch for the past few months had certainly helped, but now Laney doubted that Gwen would want to let her out of her sight.

That's why this lunch was so important, Laney thought, as she looped her arm through Gwen's.

Her mother, who had done some business with Austin in the past, knew more about the man than she did. Although Laney wasn't the gossiping type, she'd hoped to learn something—anything!—that she could tuck away for the future. Just in case he decided to try to take her baby.

Laney shuddered inwardly. Uncovering the dirt on Austin would make debating the difference between calico and chintz with Gwen a whole lot easier to stomach when they went shopping.

The sun poked out from around the clouds, warming her cheeks with the kind of low heat that made one yearn for summer. "I don't know about this, Mom," Laney said, using one hand to shield her eyes. "Do you really think it's a good idea for me to be out in public?"

"Nonsense. You can't hide forever."

Laney frowned and stopped walking. "But the family has had enough publicity lately and—"

Gwen reached for her daughter's hand. "What have I always taught you?"

Laney grasped it and held on tight. "To hold my head high and keep my back straight, no matter what I was facing."

"That's right," Gwen responded, giving her hand a firm squeeze. "We Browards never back down from a challenge—or a fight."

Before Laney could say another word, Gwen gave her an encouraging smile, opened the door and steered her inside.

The restaurant was elbow-to-elbow crowded. Strange for a Monday morning, Laney thought.

As the waiter led them to a table in the back of the room, a few people looked up as she passed by. But to her relief, nobody laughed and nobody pointed.

Still when they were seated, Laney immediately opened up her menu and nearly buried her face in it.

"You see? That wasn't so bad!" Gwen said brightly.

Laney lowered the menu slightly and peered over it. "Who are all these people?" she asked in a half whisper. The table next to them was empty, but she still didn't want anyone to hear her.

Gwen took a pair of reading glasses from her purse. "Tourists, mostly," she replied in a normal tone. "Most of them just passing through to get a look at the place that Samara Lionne wants to call home." She squinted at her daughter. "You really haven't been in town that much, have you?"

Laney shook her head. "I've been trying to keep a low profile. If I'm not at the home, most days I'm down in Bozeman in school. We only have a few more weeks until the spring session ends," she added.

Gwen slipped her glasses on. "What do you plan to do when that happens?"

Laney stared so hard at the menu that the words began to blur. "I'm not sure. I want to finish my master's degree, but I don't know how I can, now that—"

She bit the words back, but they still seared her insides.

I'm going to be a single mom.

Her mother set her own menu aside and pushed her glasses up the bridge of her nose. "I'll help you in any way I can." She reached over and pushed the menu down and away from Laney's face, so she could see her eyes. "You know that, don't you?"

Laney put the menu on the table and nodded, feeling safe in the warmth of her mother's love. "Thank you, Mom. It really means the world to me to know that I have your support."

The waiter drifted by with two glasses of water and a carafe of coffee.

While her mother perused the menu, his eyes drifted down to her belly and Laney's face got hot. Obviously, he had heard the news. It was written all over his smug grin.

Laney glared at the waiter until he looked away, but the warm feelings she was trying desperately to hold on to quickly evaporated into a deep sense of shame.

For the sake of her child, Laney made a conscious effort to quickly rid her mind of any bad feelings about her pregnancy. It was hard, but she was getting better at it day by day.

She wasn't perfect and even though the child wasn't

created under what society viewed as the ideal circumstance, her baby deserved nothing less than unconditional love.

After Gwen told the waiter her selections, Laney curtly placed her own order. He promptly scooped up their menus, leaving nothing for Laney to hide behind.

She placed her napkin on her lap and bit her lip. "Is Dad still mad at me?"

Gwendolyn shook her head. "I don't think 'mad' is the way to put it. You're his only daughter and he loves you. He only wants the best for you."

Laney's heart sank. "I realize that this is an uncomfortable situation for everyone, but I'm going to do my best to raise this child so you and Dad will be proud of me."

"Honey, we already are," Gwen replied with a reassuring smile. "And we'll be there every step of the way."

Laney poured some coffee, trying to buy time and figure out a way to ask her mom about Austin without seeming interested in him.

Gwen gently dropped two sugar cubes into her cup and stirred. "I've been meaning to ask you. How's your new equine manager working out?"

"Trey? He's very capable. I'm so glad you recommended him to me."

"Me, too. If Austin hadn't come into the picture, Trey would have been perfect for you. He's cute and he loves horses!"

Laney raised her cup to hide a smile. "When did you become a matchmaker?"

Gwen sat back in her chair. "When I noticed you were moping around the BWB like a cow too lazy to even graze," she replied matter-of-factly.

"Mom, I wasn't moping," Laney insisted. "I was fighting bouts of morning sickness and I didn't want you to know."

Gwen took a sip of coffee. "I'm still amazed that I didn't have the slightest inkling that you were sick. You could give Samara a lesson or two in acting."

At the sound of Samara's name, Laney made a face. "No, thanks. I think I'll stick to breeding horses."

"Me, too," Gwen replied and the two women laughed.

"Mom, I just want to make it clear that Austin is not in the picture."

Gwen tapped her teaspoon lightly against the cup, as if she were calling a meeting of her book club to order. "I disagree. He's the father of your child. What more would you want?"

Laney took a deep breath. It was a good question. What did she want from Austin?

"Absolutely nothing," Laney replied in a tone that sounded more confident than she really felt. "And I told him that yesterday. I suspect he's already high-tailed it back to Dallas where he belongs."

"Really?" Her mother raised a brow, which usually meant that she knew a juicy bit of gossip. "I heard he's still in Granger."

Laney's eyes widened, and it wasn't at the food that the waiter had just set before them.

"Mom, it's not even noon. How could you have learned that so quickly?"

Gwen laughed. "Honey, you know how it is around Granger. News travels fast—especially when it involves a gorgeous single man."

Laney picked up a fork and stared down at her French omelet. It sounded delicious on the menu, but the growing knot in her stomach made it look like something had died on her plate.

"My friend Betty," Gwen continued in a conspiratorial tone. "You know the one who sells real estate? She got a call from someone she knows who told her that Austin was seen around town last night looking at rental properties."

"You mean one of those hotels that are pseudo-apartments where you can get a weekly rate?" she asked.

"No, I'm talking about actual houses, Laney. It looks like he's going to be staying for more than a week. How do you feel about that?"

She carefully set her fork down. "I'm not sure."

The truth was that she didn't like it. Not one bit.

She twisted her napkin in her lap and wished she could confess to her mother that she hated the idea. That she was afraid Austin would take her baby away. But she didn't want Gwen to think that she couldn't handle the situation. That she couldn't handle being around Austin.

"Doesn't he have better things to do than hang around Granger?"

"I'm sure he does. But at least he's making an effort."

She eyed Laney's plate and frowned. "Eat your omelet. The protein is good for the baby."

Laney picked up her fork and stabbed at her eggs. "Do you have any idea where in Granger he is looking?"

"I'm not sure exactly, but Betty says he's looking at homes that have stables. I wouldn't be surprised if he brought some of his horses up here."

Laney set her fork down again, her appetite now totally gone. It sounded like Austin was making some big changes very quickly and that could only spell trouble for her.

"What's wrong, honey?"

"When is the last time you met with Austin?" she blurted.

Gwen chewed and swallowed. "Late last spring. Just before you left to travel to London. Why?"

"I ran into him there," Laney recalled. "He never said anything about moving to Granger."

"Probably because he had no reason to move here. Now he does."

"I bet his family won't approve. Do you know them?"

"Actually, I don't. I know they're well-off, like we are, but they deal in oil. We deal in cattle," Gwen said proudly. "Do you think he's told them?"

Laney paused. "I don't know."

"Perhaps because he wants you two to be together when he does." Gwen clapped her hands. "I'll bet they'll be as tickled pink as we are about their new grandbaby!"

But Laney barely heard her mom's enthusiasm. She was still stuck on the words *be together*. That was something that would never happen with her and Austin.

She felt her phone vibrating in her purse. Earlier that morning, she'd hopped on the internet and done some initial research on child custody laws in Montana. Just before her mother picked her up, she'd placed a call to an attorney in Bozeman.

She'd deliberately avoided getting the Browards' family lawyer involved to avoid causing alarm. One call to him would have resulted in an immediate call to her father, something she absolutely did not want. Their relationship was already strained enough.

When Laney finally managed to dig her phone out, her breath caught in her throat. There was a text and a voice mail from Austin.

For a moment, she was touched by the fact that he'd kept her number all these months, as she had kept his. Like a lovesick teenager, she'd dreamed of hearing his voice and talking for hours.

But now, despite her feelings for him, she had no reason to trust him. At least her dreams couldn't disappoint her.

She couldn't listen to the voice mail in front of her mom, so she read the text.

Still in town. Need to discuss next steps. See you at your place @ 2.

How dare he tell her when they were going to meet, as if she were just waiting around for his instructions?

Laney started to text:

I'm not available. Go back to Dallas.

She was about to hit the send button when Gwen tapped her fork against her cup.

"Put your phone down and eat, Laney," Gwen admonished. "Maybe the reason why you're not showing is because you don't eat."

Laney dropped her phone back into her purse. She cut some of the omelet, brought it to her lips, took one whiff and set it down.

"I can't, Mom. I'm just not feeling well. Can we go shopping tomorrow?"

Gwen frowned and motioned for the waiter. "Of course. I thought you were over your morning sickness."

"I am. But it must be stress from everything that's happened."

"Does the source of that stress start with the letter *A?*" she asked, handing the money for their meal to the waiter.

Laney didn't have to say a word, because her mother already knew the answer.

Gwen linked her arm through her daughter's as they walked out the door. "Just talk to him, honey."

But what her mother didn't understand was that she couldn't talk to, let alone be with, a man she didn't trust.

Austin wiped his boots on the porch mat, raised his right hand and paused, his knuckles mere inches from the door of Laney's home.

What do you say to a woman whom you've slept with, who is now the mother of your child and who wants nothing to do with you?

It was a question he'd been wrangling with all night, and he still didn't have the answer.

The only thing he did know was that he was glad she was back in his life.

Austin dropped his hand and checked his appearance in a decorative copper sun that hung on the white clapboard, just above the red mailbox.

He knew he was good-looking, but he wasn't vain, especially when his face reflected back at him hideously bloated like he was staring into a funhouse mirror. Or when a woman like Laney didn't fall to her knees when he walked into the room.

He grinned. He liked that about her, preferring a woman who was a little more of a challenge.

So stop being such a wimp, he told himself as he lifted his hand and rapped on the door.

The porch boards creaked as he quickly stepped

away. He waited a moment and cocked his ear, listening for her footsteps. But all he heard was the wind and the beating of his heart.

For a moment, he almost turned away and left. There was so much that he and Laney needed to work out. He knew it was going to be difficult. But even the thought of abandoning his child racked him with guilt.

He knocked once more. Nothing.

She's not going to get rid of me that easily. I have to find a way to get through to her, he thought.

He'd heard that folks rarely locked their doors in Granger. Although he found that to be a little strange, there was also something intriguing about a town whose residents could be so trusting.

He reached for the doorknob and twisted. It gave and the door opened slightly, but he decided against going in.

Austin was just about to knock one last time when he heard a male voice.

"Can I help you?"

He turned around slowly. Driving in, he'd seen two pickup trucks near the stables. Sadly, he didn't know which, if any, was Laney's, so he assumed they belonged to workers.

Now, watching the way this man walked up the porch stairs as if he owned each and every nail, it suddenly occurred to Austin that Laney could have a boyfriend, even though she'd claimed yesterday that she hadn't been with anyone else.

The thought of someone else touching her made something akin to jealousy spread through his body like spilled ink.

The man was about his age, but not nearly his height. His looks? Austin would need a woman to judge that, but the guy had the attitude of a city-born rebel. He leaned against the bannister and glared at Austin, as if he were an intruder.

So much for a warm Granger welcome.

Austin forced a tight smile. "I'm looking for Laney Broward."

When the man didn't answer immediately, he stuck out his hand. "My name's Austin. What's yours?"

"Trey."

His voice had a surly edge and he placed a booted foot on the top step of the porch, as if staking a claim, and didn't move any farther, making Austin go to him.

Austin noted Trey's firm but reluctant grip and he got the sense that he was being evaluated.

"She's tending to the horses," Trey said, pushing himself off the banister so hard that it rattled. "Excuse me."

Austin stared at him a second, stepped out of his way and watched in astonishment as Trey walked right into the house and slammed the door.

"Nice meeting you, too!" he called out, his voice dripping with sarcasm.

He took a deep breath and adjusted his Stetson. As he was walking around the corner of the house, he spotted Laney leading a chestnut thoroughbred out of the stable.

She looked up and although he was still too far away to see the expression on her face, he could tell by her tense stance that she wasn't happy to see him.

Austin took his time as he ambled toward her, his boots crunching gravel. There was no need for her to know how anxious he was to see her again.

His heart drummed with anticipation in his chest, as if he were a soldier arriving home and seeing his woman for the first time in ages.

However, Austin's excitement waned when Laney abruptly turned away and continued walking to the paddock. His hope that her unpleasant attitude toward him would soften overnight was wishful thinking.

Apparently, she needed more time. He had time, but he wouldn't wait for her forever. This was one challenge she wouldn't win.

He was only a few feet away from her when Laney slammed the paddock gate closed. Her long dark hair flowed around her face as she tried to secure it, supposedly to try to keep him out of the arena, but the bolt wouldn't catch.

"Let me help you," he offered, ignoring her stony glare.

Austin reached over the wide wooden slats and folded his hand over hers. She huffed loudly and immediately snatched her hand away.

He smiled at her politely and was not offended. Instead, he saw her obvious discomfort as an opportunity. He quickly scooted inside the paddock and secured the rusty latch.

"Try as you might, Laney, you can't lock me out of your life."

Her face flushed and she stepped back and yelped when she nearly bumped into her horse. He kept his eyes trained on hers, hoping to see something in them that could explain everything he was starting to feel for her.

Gone was the glazed, soundless wonder in her eyes that had captivated him as he'd pleasured her on New Year's Eve. Instead, they blazed with the kind of intensity reserved for battle. Right now, she looked like she wanted to smack him.

All Austin wanted to do was kiss all her anger away.

His eyes dropped to her full lips, covered only with a light gloss. They drew him in like a beacon, a fleshly symbol of sleepless nights and the agony of unfulfilled need.

Her bite was so sweet.

Austin willed away the increased tightening in his groin.

He looked at his palms, which were studded with tiny bits of rust from the latch, and frowned.

"When you didn't text me back, I wasn't sure you were going to see me," he continued in a low voice, brushing his hands off on his jeans, as he kept his eyes on her.

Laney tightened her grip on the reins, visibly annoyed. "I guess I don't have much choice, do I?"

Austin plastered what he thought was his sexiest smile on his face and leaned his elbow on the fence. "Nope."

He frowned when Laney gave no outward indication that his smile affected her. Maybe he could get through to her with the help of her four-legged friend.

He nudged his chin in the direction of the horse at her side. "What's her name?"

Laney's facial expression immediately softened. "Stella Rose," she replied as she ran her fingers through the horse's mane.

He sauntered over and cautiously rubbed his hand over her glossy coat.

"She's a beauty," he said admiringly, only half referring to the horse. As if on cue, Stella Rose bobbed her head up and down in agreement.

Stella Rose tried to grab at the reins with her teeth. "And she knows it, too!" he chuckled.

After a few seconds of Laney saying, "No, Stella," and the horse refusing and playing tug-of-war instead, Laney gave up and undid the reins. Stella Rose trotted off to graze freely, leaving the two of them alone.

Laney turned her back on him and walked away. Her long, slim legs dismissed and at the same time invited his gaze. They were meant to be worshipped, rather than clothed. He wanted to peel her skinny jeans off and taste her skin against his tongue, but he feared he would never get the chance again.

She tossed the reins over the fence, and then leaned against it, crossing her booted feet at the ankles.

"What do you want, Austin?" she said, regarding him impatiently. "I'm sure you didn't come here to flirt with my horse."

He walked toward her and grinned, enjoying the way the wind played friskily in her hair, lifting the golden-brown strands here and there.

"To tell you the truth, I'd much rather flirt with you. But I'm afraid you might hog-tie me and use me as bait for the coyotes."

Laney's eyes narrowed, although he thought he detected the thrush of a smile upon her face. "That would be a waste of my time. They'd probably turn up their noses."

He chuckled again. "Oh, really? Why's that?"

She pursed her lips. "Because you'd come back to haunt them," she retorted.

The accusation hidden in her comment snagged him like a fishhook right in the gut. At that moment, he felt like an imposition, a bad memory on perpetual rewind, a mistake.

Did she regret that night? Because he sure didn't. But he wasn't ready to tell her yet.

He leaned his hip against the fence and sighed. "I'm not a ghost, Laney. I'm just a man who wants to do the right thing."

Her eyes found his, lit with some internal struggle, but then she quickly looked away with no response.

Austin reached out and touched her face gently. "We have to talk about the baby," he cajoled in a patient voice.

Laney jerked away and set her mouth in a firm line. "There's nothing to discuss. I've already made my point clear," she insisted.

Austin leaned in close, dropping his voice low. "And I told you that I could never accept not being a part of my child's life."

Laney folded her arms and tilted her hips to the side.

"I remember that. But remember this—you're always away," she accused. "And I think—"

"But I'm here *now*," he insisted firmly.

Laney shook her head slowly, as if to imply that his answer wasn't good enough.

"How long will you be in Granger?" she said cautiously.

"At least until the baby is born. Maybe longer. Once we settle on the terms of joint custody, I can plan my travel schedule around it."

She walked a few paces away and pivoted. "Austin, I don't want my child traipsing around the world like some stowaway."

He held up both hands, trying to reassure her. "I promise I won't take *our* child anywhere without checking with you first," he emphasized.

"I appreciate that," she replied flatly. "But have you given any thought as to what kind of father you would be?"

Her words, flung as knives, sliced at his heart. They felt like a condemnation and gave new life to his own doubts.

He jammed his hands into his pockets. "Dammit, Laney!" he said curtly. "At least I wouldn't be like him!"

Laney stared at him. "What are you talking about?" she asked, her tone more subdued.

"My old man." He snorted. "He never had time for me. Always traveling and cutting his next oil deal. But he always had time to miss out on everything that was important to me."

Austin glanced up at the sky, as painful childhood memories whirled through his mind like a tornado. He wished he could wipe them away so that his mind was as clear and cloudless as the sky above him, but knew that was impossible.

Birthdays had been the worst. Never knowing whether his father would be there to help him blow out the candles. He'd stopped believing his wish would come true a long time ago. By the time Austin was a teenager, he'd realized that his father would always love money more than he loved him.

"I'm going to do everything in my power to be different. I want my son or daughter to know that I value them over everything."

When Laney didn't respond, Austin leaned against the fence so hard that the wood made a loud cracking sound.

He'd just poured out his heart, at least a little bit, and now he felt like a fool.

"You don't know anything about me, other than what

you see now," he grit out low, avoiding her eyes. He was angry at himself for saying more than he should, and for thinking that Laney cared.

"And you don't know anything about me, either," she shot back.

Austin arched a brow, surprised at her tone, and he wondered if his comments had triggered some kind of unwanted memory.

He watched her dig a small hole in the ground with the edge of one heel. Her head was bent, her hair covering her face like a shroud.

"Then why don't we stop arguing and get to know each other?"

At his words, her head snapped up. Their eyes met and he drew in a breath. His heart felt raked over and raw. But something glowed hot between them. Embers of passion sparked under the ash of frustration and he felt himself harden. Never before had he wanted someone so much.

She tucked her hair behind her ear, with one hand and then the other.

"Because—" Laney paused, her eyes still on his, and in them, he saw an emotion that he recognized in himself, but wasn't often willing to admit.

She was afraid.

The wood creaked loudly as he pushed himself off the fence.

He stood in front of her, and he was oddly relieved when she remained in place.

The wind whipped some of her hair in front of her face, and he yearned to grasp its length in his hands.

Austin swallowed hard, pushing his need to touch

her aside. "Look. I won't get in the way of your life. I just want to be involved with the baby. It's important."

As soon as he uttered those words, they seemed to hang in the air, suspended like the droplets of a promise that could evaporate any moment.

But he meant every single word.

Being a father meant more than just siring an offspring. It was an opportunity to take care of someone other than himself.

If only Laney would let him.

Austin racked his brain, trying to think of some way to reason with her, when right beside him he heard the distinct sound of chewing.

Suddenly he had an idea.

"Looks like we have some company. Let's see what Stella Rose thinks, shall we?" He slid one hand into his front pocket. "Hey, girl, do you want me to stay in Granger?"

Stella's ears pricked back and forth. She chewed for a few seconds, as if considering his question, and whinnied.

Austin pumped his fist. "I'll take that as a yes!"

Stella Rose nuzzled at his hand.

"See, Laney? She agrees. I think she likes me."

Laney rolled her eyes. "That's because you slipped her a sugar cube," she accused, pointing at him.

At the light-hearted tone in her voice, Austin took a chance and quickly slipped his arm around Laney's thin waist, pulling her to him.

"How could I have done that?" he said low. "When all the sugar in the world is right here in my arms?"

Laney didn't say anything, but he felt her lean against him and he gently pulled her to him even closer. He took a section of her hair and smoothed it back over her shoulder.

"You know, Laney, I may not know your favorite color or your favorite food, but I do know the way you like to be kissed."

Before she could say another word, Austin tilted her chin up, bent down and brushed his lips over hers almost tentatively, curious to see if they felt the same as he remembered.

They were soft, pliable, but he felt something different, too. They felt like they belonged to him, and he drew her bottom lip into his mouth and sucked gently. She tasted different, too, like sun rays that couldn't be harnessed, but could burn you if you got too close. She uttered a faint moan and that was all he needed to hear. He knew she felt it, too.

Her abdomen pressed against his, somewhat awkwardly. It felt slightly rounded, like a balloon that wasn't yet fully inflated, and he was gravely aware that their child lay nestled between them. It made him feel even closer to her, and even more protective.

Austin broke away from Laney quickly, breathing hard, struggling to blot away the sudden images of her naked in his arms.

He knew he would never be content with just kissing her, but he had to move slowly. He waited until he had control of his voice, and then spoke casually, as if the kiss had never happened.

"When is your next doctor appointment?"

She gave him a curious look, and then walked over to Stella Rose, as if she were trying to distance herself, too.

"The day after tomorrow."

"Who's driving you?"

She looked at him like he was crazy. "I'm driving myself, Austin. I'm not an invalid."

"Correction, darling—I'm driving you."

She started to protest, but he walked over and laid a finger upon her lips to quiet her.

"Get used to me being around, Laney. Trust me, it'll make things easier for both of us."

He tipped his hat and as he strode away, he knew his words were a lie. By kissing Laney again, he'd just made it even harder not to fall in love with her.

Chapter 5

Laney slipped into her leather jacket and half jogged to the paddock, hoping to spend a few minutes with Stella Rose before Austin picked her up. Although he'd insisted on driving her to her prenatal checkup, she still wasn't sure if she wanted him to be so involved in her life.

She let her knapsack fall to the ground and sighed. All around the ranch, the dirt was heavily pocked by cowboy boots, horses' hooves and good old-fashioned time. When it rained, it was easy to step in a puddle and when it was dry, well, it was even easier to trip or twist an ankle.

She made a mental note to speak to Trey about getting the worst portions backfilled and raked with new soil. Making her home child-friendly required a bit more than just locks on the bottom kitchen cabinets.

She pushed open the arena gate, which was easier to operate now. Yesterday, Austin had surprised her by replacing the rusty latch with a brand-new one. He claimed that he'd read a blog article that said rust could be dangerous to the baby.

The suggestion about backfilling the ranch grounds had also been his idea, just one thing on his list to try to make Laney's home safer for the baby.

The man was full of surprises lately. Over the past several days, he'd also brought her roses, which had promptly made her sneeze, hired a prenatal massage therapist to knead her sore muscles into submission and had his own personal chef in Dallas create a special daily menu that would ensure both mother and child were eating healthy.

Laney closed the gate, not bothering to hide the smile that lit upon her face.

Austin was beginning to leave his imprint on her life, just as he did on her lips.

How can a kiss that only lasted a few moments still resonate with me days later? she thought as she walked through the ankle-high prairie grass.

She wondered if he was going to kiss her today. She hoped he would, but he seemed to be keeping a polite distance.

Laney squeezed her hand into the front pocket of her new maternity jeans, which she needed for the first time today, and drew out a couple of sugar cubes.

"Stella Rose, I think I'm in trouble!" she announced.

Her beloved horse's ears pricked forward. Laney laughed as Stella Rose briefly nuzzled her palm and then proceeded to gobble up the treat.

"You don't care, do you? As long as I keep giving you your treats," she murmured, fingering her horse's silky mane.

Laney heard a car honk, turned and spotted her mother's bright red convertible making its way up her driveway, with Brooke in the passenger seat. She gave Stella Rose one last sugar cube just as Gwen leaned out of her window.

"Are you still spoiling her?" her mother admonished in a teasing voice. "Wasn't a gold medal around her neck enough?"

"Since I can't ride her now, I want to show her how much I love her. Besides, she can't eat a medal!"

"True enough." Gwen laughed. "How are you feeling?"

Laney shrugged. "Okay, I guess. A little tired in the mornings, but no more sleeping with my cheek pressed to the bathroom floor."

Brooke grimaced. "When I get pregnant, which—" she shot her mother-in-law a warning look "—won't be for a long time, I am so not looking forward to all the icky stuff that goes along with it."

Gwen waved Brooke's comment away as she stepped out of the car. "Nonsense. God's just getting a woman ready for the greatest job on earth. There's nothing icky about that!"

Laney grinned and leaned into her mother's embrace, wondering how she always managed to be so optimistic about every situation. It was almost as if she had never experienced any pain at all. She knew that had to be impossible. But Gwen had never been anything but an unwavering pillar of strength that the entire Broward family relied upon. And Laney needed her mother more than ever now.

Brooke got out of the car and reached into the backseat. "I made you an apple pie," she announced.

She walked over and tried to thrust it into Laney's hands.

Laney's eyes widened and she inhaled the delicious aroma. "Thank you," she said, giving Brooke a quick hug. "That was so kind of you. I'm on my way out. Could you put it in the kitchen for me?"

Gwen waited until Brooke was out of earshot. "You look a lot happier than when I first saw you," she remarked. "Did you talk to Austin?"

"Yes," Laney said, slightly evasive.

"And?" said her mother. "Don't keep me hanging like somebody's drawers on a clothesline. I'm your mother, remember?"

Laney laughed out loud. "We're trying to work together."

Gwen gave her a smothering hug. "I'm so glad. Did he say how long he was staying in town?"

Laney shook her head against Gwen's neck. She didn't want to tell her that Austin had said he was going to stay until the baby was born. In her heart, she didn't believe he was going to stick around that long.

At some point, Laney feared that Austin would get bored by the small town of Granger, the prospect of being a father and most of all, her.

If Gwen was disappointed by her answer, she didn't show it. Instead, she held her daughter at arm's length.

"You look beautiful today. We came here to see if you wanted to have breakfast, but it sounds like you have other plans. Where are you headed?"

"To the doctor."

Laney watched her mother's eyes transition from admiration to concern. "It's nothing to worry about," she said hastily. "It's just time for my monthly checkup. Austin is taking me."

Gwen raised a brow. "That's good. I see he's already taking responsibility for the child, and you. He's a good man, Laney."

I don't know if he's a good man, but he's a great kisser and a whole lot more, Laney thought. But she wasn't about to tell that to her mother.

"So you'll give me a rain check on breakfast?" Gwen asked.

Laney nodded, just as Brooke walked up to them.

"Laney, you're not coming with us?"

"No. She has a doctor's appointment," her mother interjected, "and a date with Austin."

"Mom. It's not a date," Laney protested, even though a part of her wished that it was.

She and Austin had made a grand-slam home run, more than a few times, before actually walking the bases. Nothing had happened in the proper order. Everything about their so-called relationship was backward, and at this point, she wasn't even sure she could rightfully call him a friend.

Although she knew he loved it when she played with the hair on his chest. And that he liked to nuzzle at the insides of her elbows. And when he climaxed, he breathed her name into her ear over and over again like it was his lifeline to another world.

And she knew that she wanted to be his connection to something unexplained, to be his ultimate pleasure, intertwined together, for better or for worse.

The problem was that it was all wrong. They were all wrong. Wrong timing. Wrong order and, possibly, the wrong man.

The sound of her mother's voice drew her from her thoughts.

"I was hoping we could squeeze in some shopping, but we will have to go another day. Samara's Grand Ball is only a few weeks away," Gwen added.

"I don't know if I'm even going to go," Laney admitted.

Although the furor over her "baby bump" had died down, she still wanted to keep a low profile in Granger. Luckily, the media hadn't learned that Austin was the father of Laney's baby, but she wasn't sure how long that luck was going to last.

"But, Laney, you have to attend," Brooke said. "The entire family will be there."

"I agree," Gwen noted. "Samara is giving the ball for the people of Granger, it will reflect badly on the community as a whole if all of us are not there."

"And it won't make the Browards look too good, either," Laney added with a smirk.

"Laney, you know I don't cater to the whims of people's opinions," her mother scolded. "However, I do believe that sometimes it's better to bend than to be broken. No one knows why Samara is buying land here, and why other people are playing copycat, but we're not going to find out the answers by avoiding her," Gwen reasoned.

"So are you saying we should treat this event as a fact-finding mission?" Laney asked, only half joking.

"I think that's a great idea," Brooke said, surprising her. "You never know what we'll find out."

"Or what Samara will reveal," Gwen added. "I think that she will use the Ball to announce something big. Maybe she's going to make a movie here!"

Laney nodded and watched as the two women got in the car and drove away.

Her mother was right, of course. Attending the ball was the courteous thing to do. But Gwen, and even Brooke, failed to understand one simple fact—having

Laney in public, alone and pregnant at a huge social gathering, only invited more questions. Questions she wasn't quite ready to answer.

Austin drummed his fingers impatiently on the steering wheel. Other than telling him that his brand-new one-hundred-thousand-dollar Range Rover truck was "nice," Laney had handed him the address of the clinic and hadn't said a word since. That was seventy miles ago, and they still had a long way to go.

He stole a glance at his quiet passenger. Her face angled toward the window where the Montana landscape quickly rolled into memory as they traveled south on Interstate 15 to Bozeman. The golden-brown strands of her hair were tucked neatly behind her left ear and he noticed for the first time the fine line of her jaw, the impertinent chin and her long, graceful neck.

With her face in profile, she was the perfect model for a pen-and-ink artist. Although he couldn't draw anything more than crude stick figures, even if he had all the talent in the world, he'd never be able to capture the modest, understated sophistication that was Laney Broward. She was as strong and as powerful as he, but with an obliquely corralled wild streak just waiting to be unleashed. Like her prize-winning thoroughbreds, Laney was born to win, but not to be captured.

He forced his eyes back on the road where they belonged and swallowed hard, but it didn't dispel his nervousness. This was their first outing together and he wasn't sure what to say. It had all the awkwardness of a first date, he thought as he wiped one sweaty palm and then the other on his jeans, but they weren't a couple.

Over the past several days, he'd come to realize that being her friend was the only way to begin to put some sort of frame around their relationship.

Things were shaky indeed. The kiss hadn't changed that, but he had to start somewhere.

He stole a look at her belly. And even under the tunic she wore, he could tell there was an even bigger bulge there now than a few days ago when he'd kissed her. He felt his pride swelling at the life she was cultivating. A life they had created.

"If I had it my way, I'd have ridden Stella Rose all the way to Bozeman," Laney blurted out suddenly.

"Why's that?" he asked, a little stunned by her question.

"Because you've been staring at me out of the corner of your eye ever since we left my house." She turned to him. "Have I grown horns on the top of my head or something?"

"No, but your halo is looking a little tarnished lately," he replied, with a hint of a smile.

She shot him a look and he broke out laughing. "You're so much fun to tease. Just relax, would you?"

Laney slid one leg over the other and leaned back against the seat. She rolled her eyes and looked up at the ceiling of the vehicle, exposing the swell of her neck. But when she turned toward him again, she had a half smile on her lips.

"I'll try, okay?" she said. "This isn't easy."

"I know," he said with a nod. He didn't stop to wonder if she was talking about being with him or the pregnancy in general. He was just happy that she'd broken the silence between them.

He turned on SiriusXM. The station was already tuned to one that played old-school country, where a singer was crooning that he had another broken heart and he "just didn't give a damn." Austin bobbed his head to the bluesy beat, refusing to think about his past failed relationships. The important thing was that he'd moved on. He just wasn't sure at this point if Laney was the ultimate destination.

"You know what's the best recipe for a broken heart?" It was his roundabout way of finding out if she'd ever been in love.

"In my case, chocolate was always the perfect antidote," Laney said. There was a hint of snark in her voice, but no bitterness. He wanted to ask the particulars, but he knew she wouldn't appreciate the intrusion.

"No, it's remembering the single most important quality that your ex lacked, so you can make sure to find that exact quality in your next relationship."

"Okay, Dr. Phil," she said, crossing her arms and staring at him intently. "What are you looking for in a woman that your ex lacked, whomever she was?"

"Trust," Austin replied, without hesitation. "And integrity. What about you?"

Her eyes darkened momentarily. "Laughter."

Austin slanted his eyes at her and quickly returned his attention to the road.

"Don't get me wrong, trust and integrity are really important to me, too," she said hastily. "But life is too hard to be serious all the time."

"So did I ever tell you the one about the guy who met a princess in the desert?"

"No, what happened?"

"He was so thirsty for love, he drank her in like water," he replied thickly. "But in the morning, he discovered she was only a mirage."

Austin feared that's exactly what would happen to him, if he wasn't careful. The passion he'd craved and explored with Laney that one night, the horizontal, undulating waves of heat that he'd never wanted to end. He wanted to experience all of that and more again. But were the feelings he'd poured into every touch real, or were they simply an illusion of his deepest desires?

Their eyes met and they both turned away quickly. Neither wanted to be drawn into examining the meaning behind Austin's statement, nor did they wish to confirm the existence of their attraction to each other.

But it was there fluttering between them, as a question and as a fact.

"Austin, that's not funny," replied Laney, staring straight ahead. "That's depressing."

"You're right," he said, a bit sheepishly. "It must be this darn music." He reached over and switched to the comedy station. A good joke or two was something they both needed to release the tension and bind the wounds that lay hidden in their hearts.

An hour and a half later, Austin was perched on a circular stool next to Laney, who lay stretched out on an examination table.

He felt blessed to even be in the room, and was still reeling with surprise that Laney wanted him there, with her, during the exam.

The sonographer had her back turned to the couple as she readied her supplies.

The walls were painted a gender-generic beige likely meant to calm, but the effect was undermined by the colorful Jackson Pollock print, which led to equal amounts of confusion.

At least to him. He never got Pollock. His paintings always looked as though they were done by a three-year-old who'd overdosed on Kool-Aid.

Laney shivered a little.

He touched her arm lightly. "Are you okay? Do you need another blanket?"

She shook her head. "Just a little nervous."

Laney was dressed in a blue pinstriped hospital gown covering her top, and a flimsy blue paper blanket covering below her belly. Every other part of her beneath the gown and blanket was bare.

He tried not to think about that little detail. Instead, he reached for her hand and entwined her fingers with his, and gave a little squeeze. "You look beautiful, you know that?" he whispered in her ear.

He watched her chest rise as she took a deep breath and turned toward him, a grateful smile on her face.

The sonographer approached the table. "I did warm this up for you so you'll be a little more comfortable," she said, as she squirted a clear, jellylike substance on Laney's abdomen.

Austin released Laney's hand and watched, fascinated. "What is that stuff?" he asked, not caring if he sounded ignorant.

The sonographer smiled patiently. "It's a special gel that helps the ultrasound waves travel directly through the skin to the part I'm imaging." She grabbed a white wandlike tool attached by a cord to a computer. "This transducer sends and receives the sound waves. The image of the baby will be displayed on the monitors in just a few moments."

Austin and Laney looked up at a flat-screen monitor suspended from the ceiling.

The sonographer turned her head and looked at the computer monitor, while continuing to move the transducer slowly over Laney's abdomen.

A few seconds later, Austin hitched in a breath. In a fluid yet grainy black-and-white, he saw the perfectly formed shape of a tiny human being.

His child.

"Do you see the baby?" Laney asked, excitedly.

"Yes," he replied, awestruck. "It's beautiful!"

Mesmerized by the image before him, he reached for Laney's hand again without taking his eyes from the screen.

"Can we see if it's a boy or a girl?" he asked, his eyes glued to the screen.

The sonographer paused midstream. "It's a little early in the pregnancy to see the sex of the baby, but we could try. It's up to you, ma'am," she said.

Laney slipped her hand from his and turned to him. Somehow, he managed to tear his eyes away from the monitor. She shook her head. "No, Austin. I don't want to know. I want it to be a surprise for us and for the family. Besides, I promised Mama. No more secrets," she said, emphatically. "Plus, it will be fun to choose names for the baby," she added quickly.

"No more secrets," Austin repeated with a nod. "Got it. That's fine, honey."

Honey.

He looked down at his lap briefly. The endearment had slipped out before he could catch it, but the word fit. Laney was sweet to look at and even sweeter to taste.

Austin lifted his head and cast a quick glance at her, but she didn't seem to be perturbed, and he breathed an internal sigh of relief.

"Austin Jr. has a mighty nice ring to it, doesn't it?" he advised in a serious tone.

Laney narrowed her eyes. "Now hold on just a minute." But before she had a chance to argue, the doctor stepped into the room. He was a short, squat, nearly bald man.

"Dr. McCreedy, this is Austin Johns. The father of my baby."

Austin stood and shook his hand. "Pleased to meet you."

The doctor washed his hands and then walked to the other side of the examination table and stuck his stethoscope in his ears. He pressed it over Laney's heart. Suddenly, he knit his brows together.

"Austin Johns, your name sounds familiar. Do you happen to own a racehorse by the name of The Perfect Shot?"

Austin nodded. "That's right."

He grinned wide. "That horse made me a ton of money a few years back. I haven't seen him on the circuit lately. What's he doing?"

Austin grinned back. "Semi-retired. He's a stud now."

The doctor shook his head ruefully. "Lucky animal. Wish I were, too," he replied.

Laney and Austin both laughed as he squirted some more goop on Laney's abdomen and grabbed the transducer.

"Let's see if we can hear a heartbeat today, shall we?"

Austin felt his eyes widen. "Wow, you can actually hear it with that device?"

"Yep, it's definitely more powerful than these old things," Dr. McCreedy said, quickly draping his stethoscope around his neck. He leaned back and turned up the volume on the ultrasound station.

Laney twisted her head toward Austin. "We tried at my last appointment, but the baby wasn't in the right position."

She held his eyes and they both held their breath as the doctor watched the monitor and slowly moved the transducer over her belly.

Suddenly, from out of nowhere and deep within bloomed the most wonderful sound in the world.

The sound of life.

"There it is," Dr. McCreedy murmured softly. "There it is."

To Austin, the baby's heartbeat sounded like a band of galloping horses. Percussive, full of energy and so profound that it moved him to tears.

He saw tears glistening in Laney's eyes, too, and it was all he could do not to kiss her on the mouth.

I wish we were alone right now, he thought.

Dr. McCreedy removed the transducer and the room went stark quiet. Austin and Laney said nothing as they both tried to preserve the sound of their baby's heartbeat somewhere deep within their memory.

"Everything is looking and sounding good," the doctor said. "Are there any concerns that I can address?"

Laney looked at the doctor and shook her head, but Austin touched her arm.

"I have two, actually," he blurted out. "How soon can we do a DNA test for paternity?" Somehow he was able to ask the question without faltering, even though he knew it would hurt Laney deeply.

Dr. McCreedy scrunched up his brows and his eyes traveled from Laney to Austin and back to his patient again.

"You're now in your second trimester, seventeenth week. At this point, we could perform an amniocentesis, which is where we insert a very thin needle through your abdomen and into your uterus and take a small amount of amniotic fluid, which we can test for paternity. There are risks, the biggest of them being miscarriage, which I know, Laney, you were concerned about previously."

"Miscarriage?" Austin felt his heart lurch. "What are you talking about?"

Dr. McCreedy turned to his patient. "Do you want me to share the details with him?" When she nodded her consent, he continued. "Laney came into my office a few weeks ago after an episode of spotting. She was concerned that she might have miscarried the baby. We did an ultrasound and examined her and all was well. However, I did request that she stop riding for the duration of her pregnancy, and advised as much rest as possible. For physical activity, I authorized light yoga and tai chi, both of which are safe and highly effective."

Austin swallowed back his fear. If Laney had lost the baby, he wouldn't be sitting here with her right now. Even worse, he might have never even known that he'd gotten her pregnant.

"So what do you recommend about the testing, Doctor?"

"Wait until the baby is born," Dr. McCreedy answered firmly. "Then establish paternity when there are no risks for the mother or the child."

Austin nodded, ignoring Laney's accusing eyes.

The doctor got up to wash his hands. "What's your second concern?" he asked.

"I know Laney has established a relationship with you, but I'm wondering if she should have a doctor closer to Granger, in case of an emergency."

Laney started to protest but stopped when Dr. Mc-Creedy turned to the couple from the sink.

"I think that's an excellent idea. I'll have my secretary give you the name of one of my colleagues in Helena."

He dried his hands and handed Laney a towel. Austin presumed it was so that she could wipe all the goo off her abdomen.

"Good luck to you both and feel free to call me with any additional concerns."

When the doctor exited, Austin left the room, too, so Laney could get changed. He knew she was mad at him again. He'd decided to wait on asking her if she would have told him about the baby if, God forbid, she had suffered a miscarriage. He wasn't sure he could handle the answer.

On their way out, the secretary handed them the name of the referral doctor and a brochure on birthing methods. Although he'd heard of natural childbirth classes, the only thing he knew was that they involved a lot of heavy breathing. He wanted to help Laney in any way he could, but now he wasn't sure if she would accept his assistance during labor.

When they got to the car, Laney finally spoke.

"How could you even think you're not the father? After what we shared that night?" She turned away and pulled on the door handle, but it wouldn't open. He hadn't unlocked it yet. "Let me in, please."

"No," he said, slipping the keys back into his pocket. "Not until you give me a chance to explain why I asked about the DNA testing."

She backed up against the car and crossed her arms. He shifted uncomfortably.

"I didn't mean to hurt you, Laney. I just need to prove I'm the father for legal purposes."

"And you think that doesn't hurt me? Trying to take away my child?"

He shook his head. "Take away? No! You've got it all wrong. I want to provide for the baby, and for you, for your entire lives."

Laney pressed her lips together before speaking. Her tone was softer than he'd expected. "I told you before, Austin. I don't need your money. I need your—"

Suddenly she turned her face away, and refused to look at him.

Austin quickly stepped in front of her, leaned his hand against the car and guided her cheek back to center. "What do you need, Laney?" He pressed his forehead lightly against hers. "What do you need?" he repeated. "I'd give you anything you want. Anything at all."

Laney wouldn't meet his eyes, and instead slipped under his arm, and his heart clenched when she back-pedaled a few steps away.

"I need space, Austin."

Her voice was firm, and although he didn't want to believe that her words were true, it was against his nature to beg.

"Fine," he muttered, dropping his hands to his sides. "But you need to know one thing. That baby means everything to me."

They rode in silence the whole way back. No comedy, no country music, and with Laney thankfully dozing beside him, no arguing.

Upon arriving at her home, he gently nudged her elbow to wake her up. When she did, he was pleased to see a half smile on her face. Yet he feared it was the result of a nice dream, rather than meant for him, so he said nothing.

What was there to say? He was doing exactly what she claimed she wanted. He was giving her space. For now. Because he wasn't sure how long he would last without being close to her in some way.

Before Laney stepped out of the car, she reached into her purse, pulled something out and shoved it toward him.

When he saw what it was, his heart dropped into his stomach.

"The doctor gave me two," Laney muttered, thrusting her hand out.

"Thank you," he managed, his voice catching in his throat as he accepted the grainy black-and-white sonogram image of their baby.

Laney shut the door and walked away without another word.

Austin stared after her a moment, still shocked. He knew she could have kept both copies for herself, but instead she chose to give one to him.

His eyes dropped to the image again, hoping that Laney's gesture was a sign that she was starting to accept him as part of their child's life. But at that moment, it didn't matter because in his hands, he held a physical reminder of his future, and he knew his life would never be the same again.

Chapter 6

Laney took an old bandanna from the back of her jeans pocket, stuck her pitchfork in the packed dirt and wiped her brow. Trey had gone into town for some additional feed for the horses and she had just started to put some new hay in Stella Rose's stall.

It had been several days since she'd seen Austin, and she missed him more than she was willing to admit. Although deep down, she was glad that he'd ignored her request for space.

Since taking her to the doctor, he'd stopped by with a bunch of flowers, groceries (always fresh fruit and vegetables) and the latest bestselling paperbacks. He always asked how she felt and if she needed anything else to make her life more comfortable.

At first, accepting his help would rile her inside just a little. She valued her independence so much that it almost seemed impossible to think of sharing her life with someone.

Laney smiled. She was beginning to think that her mother was right. Austin was a good man, and he was proving it more and more every day. She was beginning to realize that maybe she was the problem. That maybe she couldn't handle him.

Due to her commitment to her equestrian career, her other relationships had been few and far between. She was never able to truly connect with any man. There was always something that felt "off."

But with Austin, things felt different. It helped tremendously that the playing field was level. They both loved horses, had plenty of ambition and enough money that they would never have to work again, if they so chose. At an emotional level, she didn't know how he felt about her, and he didn't know how she felt about him.

She was still trying to figure things out, and where Austin fit in her life, other than being the father of her child. The man occupied much of her thoughts and was starting to wheedle his way into her heart, too.

Laney sighed and was just about to reach for the pitchfork and toss another fresh pile of hay into the stall when someone grabbed it away from behind her.

"What do you think you're doing?"

She recognized the voice immediately. "Austin! Would you stop sneaking up on me?" she exclaimed, whirling around to face him. "I'm just taking care of my horse."

She reached for the pitchfork, but Austin held it above his head and out of her reach.

"Didn't you hear what Dr. McCreedy said?" Austin demanded. "Tai chi and yoga were his recommended forms of exercise. I'm pretty sure mucking out a horse stall doesn't qualify."

"I think you're overreacting," Laney fumed, reaching for the tool again. "I appreciate your concern, but I can handle this task. I've been doing it for years."

She bit her lip, refusing to start an argument with him, as she inwardly tried to let go of her need to control everything. A part of her feared that the only reason he was probably concerned about her was for the welfare of his child. She knew it was an awful way to feel, but she wished that he cared about her as a woman, not simply as a vessel for his offspring.

The fact was that since he'd arrived in Granger, he'd never said a word about establishing a permanent relationship with her. All he talked about was his desire to work out a joint custody agreement. He was probably doing nice things for her to bait her into believing he cared, when he really didn't.

What did she expect from a man who, as far as she knew, was more interested in making money than in building a full-time life with her and their child?

Laney lifted her chin slightly, deciding that she wouldn't be his means to an end, because for her that meant a broken heart.

He's trying to change.

She pushed her thoughts away and reached for the tool again, but he still wouldn't let her have it. Instead, he turned and walked away, pitchfork in hand.

"Wait here," he said.

She crossed her arms and watched as he disappeared into the stable office and brought out a folding chair.

Austin set it down in front of her and pointed. "You. Sit and watch me work," he commanded, leaning the pitchfork against the stall.

She shook her head stubbornly and refused. That is, until he unbuttoned his denim shirt. At the sight of his muscular arms, she sank down into the chair. The metal felt cool, but the man standing before her was hot, hot, hot.

Once seated, she was glad she was there. She hadn't

realized how tired she was, and how amazing he looked without his shirt. She almost laughed with the realization of how little she'd seen of his body in the daytime.

"Hold this, will you?" he asked, tossing her his shirt. "I'd hang it up somewhere but I don't want it to get dirty."

Laney caught it easily, despite being distracted by the sight of his bronzed skin. Now she had to fight the urge to smell his shirt.

She fanned herself lightly, telling herself the reason why was because it was an unusually warm spring day.

As she gazed at him, the pull of desire coupled with the momentary release of her fears. It seemed so natural being there with Austin, watching as he effortlessly pitched hay into the stall.

Minutes later, he finished and hadn't even broken a sweat.

"How's that?" he asked, gesturing toward his work.

She crossed her legs and looked at the stall with a critical eye. "It's okay. But Stella Rose likes her bedding a little thicker in the back corner."

That wasn't totally true but it gave her the chance to watch some more of Austin's amazing muscles do a midday workout.

Austin nodded and turned around.

Laney put her elbow on her knee and hid a smile behind her hand as he stabbed some hay with the pitchfork.

He stepped farther into the stall. "Guess who stopped by my house the other day?" he said, his back to her.

"Who?" Laney asked distractedly, her eyes soaking him in like he was a rare sculpture.

"Your mother."

Her stomach lurched and she dropped her hand away from her face. "Really? What did she want?"

"She told me about the ball that Samara is throwing for the town." He turned and leaned one shoulder against the wall. "And in not so many words, she urged me to take you."

Laney felt her cheeks burn with embarrassment. Her matchmaking mom was at it again.

She leaned forward in her seat, waiting for the rest of the story, but he only hung the pitchfork on the wall near the stable doors. Then he went to a nearby sink, washed and dried his hands.

When he was done, she got up from her seat and did the same.

"And what did you say to her?" she asked.

Austin shrugged and folded up the chair. "I told her I already had a date," he replied nonchalantly.

Once a player, always a player, Laney thought as she felt her heart drop into her stomach in disappointment.

"Whom, if I may ask, are you taking to the Granger Ball?" she asked. Her tone sounded a little too casual in her ears. She actually cared very deeply about his answer.

Austin leaned against a nearby wall and grinned. "Stella Rose. Do you think she'll go with me now that I made her bed?" he asked, with a mischievous wink.

Laney's exhale was a mixture of relief and minor annoyance. Austin seemed to love to get her riled up over nothing, and she fell for it every time.

Still, she had difficulty holding back a smile as she walked over and tossed Austin's shirt in his face.

He caught it in midair. "What did you do that for?"

"Because you know well and good you can't take a

horse to an event like that. If you didn't want to take me, just say so. Don't make me look like a fool in front of my mother!"

Although Laney loved being in her stable, suddenly she needed fresh air. She marched swiftly outside and sat down on a bench underneath a pine tree next to her unplanted vegetable garden.

Austin trotted out after her. "I'm sorry. I was only trying to make you laugh."

She gave him a half smile. "I know. I don't know why I've been so sensitive lately."

"I read in an article that pregnancy makes some women more emotional." He touched her hand. "At least I'm not making you cry."

Not yet, she thought, and then immediately pushed the negative thought away.

Give him a chance.

"At any rate, I would love to take you to the ball. And that is not a joke. I'm totally serious."

"Too late," Laney sniffed.

He plopped down beside her. "Why? I said I was sorry."

"No. That's not it at all. You're too late. I decided not to go weeks ago."

Laney was more certain than ever that attending the ball would be a mistake, for both of them.

"Besides, do you remember what happened the last time I attended a gala event and you were present?" she blurted.

As soon as she spoke the words, she regretted them. His eyes sought hers, and the hunger she saw in them could not be mistaken, nor could it be satisfied.

"I remember, Laney. Do you? Do you really remember?"

All the time, she thought. The night they'd spent together haunted her days, and turned her heart upside-down.

"Can I show you something?" he asked.

Austin brought out his wallet and took out the sonogram picture of their baby. He'd had it laminated, but it was already looking a little crinkly and worn.

"You gave me this picture, but I know that you didn't have to. Why did you?"

Her eyes met his. "Because I knew you would treasure it."

Austin placed his hands gently on her stomach, so gently she could barely breathe. She could feel the heat of his palms through her shirt.

"Laney, do you realize what a gift you've given me? You've given me a chance to live outside myself."

She tilted her head in confusion. "What do you mean?"

He looked down at his lap, and then back up at her. "I've been so wrapped up in my life lately. It's nice to focus on something else."

She felt tears burn behind her eyes and she stood up abruptly. If she ever needed to know how Austin felt about her, he'd just made it very clear with that one statement. All he cared about was the baby.

Laney fought back a sudden wave of jealousy, willing herself not to cry. So what if he cared about the baby more than her? At least her child would know its father.

I'm jealous of my own baby? My hormones must really be out of whack, she suddenly thought, railing herself with guilt internally.

She walked a few paces away, trying to ignore the tightening in her chest and the distinctly unmotherly feelings that assailed her mind.

Austin stood. "Your mother also asked if I was going to have a nursery at my house, too," he said, a bit awkwardly. "Laney, I think that's best, don't you?"

"No, Austin. I don't think so," she responded irritably. "If I don't want our baby traipsing around the world, I sure don't want him or her sleeping in an unfamiliar crib."

"It wouldn't be unfamiliar," he reasoned. "The baby needs to get used to my home, as well as yours."

"Trust me, Austin. You don't want a baby to wake you up at 3:00 a.m."

She turned her back on him and walked away. Austin obviously had no idea what was entailed in being a parent. Neither did she, but at least she could be realistic. There would be lots of dirty diapers and not a lot of sleep.

But Laney didn't care. She couldn't wait to hold her baby in her arms, even if she had to spend every night alone.

Austin jogged up next to her. "I'm a breeder, remember? I've had horses wake me up and keep me up earlier than that."

Laney stopped in her tracks and shook her head. "It wouldn't work, Austin."

He touched her shoulder briefly and she turned around.

"Sure it would," Austin insisted. "He or she will get the best of both worlds. Two bedrooms, each decorated differently, with loads of toys—"

"And two parents living apart," Laney cried out, raising her hands in hurt and frustration "What more could a kid want?"

She turned away, sick of trying to pretend that things could work out between them. The picture of joint custody he was trying to draw only made her stomach knot with anxiety, especially since it was clear that he didn't want a real relationship with her.

"Hey." Austin reached for her arm and she turned around reluctantly. "I didn't ask for this," he said harshly.

"I didn't, either," she cautioned, trying to keep her voice and her nerves steady. His fingers felt hot and insistent against her skin.

Austin looked deep into her eyes, and she saw that he wasn't going to give in so easily.

"You gave me that picture for a reason. You know I deserve a chance to be a father to my child, don't you?"

Laney opened her mouth, but no words came at first. Was it worth it to try to argue anymore?

"I only wish—" She paused and took a deep breath, debating whether to tell him one of the reasons she was initially upset about the pregnancy.

She pulled away from Austin's grasp, hoping at the same time she could escape the hold he was starting to have on her heart.

Austin released her arm. "What do you wish, Laney? Please tell me."

Whether he meant it or not, she didn't know, but the urgent concern in his voice gave her the courage to go on.

"It's silly, really, and very old-fashioned," she started, her chin lowered as she kicked away some pebbles with her cowboy boots. "Although I'm excited about being a mom, I only wish I'd gone about it in the proper way, in the right order. Like my mom and dad did." She stared up at him. "Is that so wrong?"

Austin shook his head. "We can't change what we did. All we can do is deal with the outcome the best we can." He paused and swallowed. "Tell me something, Laney. That time you thought you'd had a miscarriage. If you had lost the baby, would you ever have told me that you were pregnant? Or would you have let me live my whole life not knowing that I had lost a child?"

His question struck her at the center of her moral fiber, and she struggled to remain calm. "How could you even think such a thing?"

Austin crossed his arms. "Easy. I had to find out you were pregnant through a newspaper headline, rather than from your own lips."

"I had every intention of telling you," she replied, knowing that he had a right to be angry. "When the time was right."

"The problem is that nobody knew when that would be but you," he said, and there was no mistaking the veil of mistrust in his eyes.

Laney shook her head and walked away, both sad and hurt that he hadn't forgiven her for keeping the baby a secret.

Austin caught up with her, reached out, stopping her again in her tracks.

He suddenly drew her into his arms, nearly knocking the breath out of her. He cupped her cheeks in his hands, forcing her to look up at him. "Did you ever have something that you didn't know you needed, didn't even know that you wanted, and have it taken away?"

She shook her head, her heart pounding inside her chest, and his palms felt tantalizingly rough against her skin. She felt something bead within her, strung low and hot. "I don't know what you're talking about, Austin."

His eyes searched hers with the kind of passion that was completely honorable. "That's what this baby means to me. You may not believe this, but I'm not just all about money and business, and I can prove it to you. If you'll only let me." His voice hardened, and she knew that he was running out of patience. "But you have to tell me the truth. No more secrets. If our baby had died, would you ever have told me?"

Laney broke away from his embrace. "Yes!" she shouted roughly, so hurt by his distrust in her that she could barely breathe. "Now leave me alone. This discussion is over. I think it's better if we communicate through our attorneys from now on."

Without another word, she ran into the house and slammed the door so hard that the plates in her kitchen cabinet rattled. She paused and listened to see if Austin would follow her, and when he didn't, she walked slowly up the stairs to her bedroom.

Lying across the bed, she stared up at the ceiling and wondered if she'd made the right choice by telling him the truth. Even worse, if he didn't believe her, it would make sharing custody of their child even that much more difficult.

Chapter 7

Austin hooked his thumbs into the back pockets of his jeans and stared after Laney in sad amazement. She'd run away from him again. The thunderous sound of her slamming the back door echoed in his mind, and he felt as if she'd kicked the door to her heart closed, too.

Perhaps permanently.

He leaned against the pine tree for a few minutes, inhaling its heady scent to try to clear his head, before ambling away from her house toward his car, lost in his thoughts.

Was she telling the truth?

He shoved his hands in his pockets and walked on, desperately trying to believe that she had planned to tell him about the baby, miscarriage or not. If only he knew why she'd waited for months to tell him. Why had she kept their child a secret for so long?

In the distance, Stella Rose neighed and he stopped in his tracks. The wind whipped through his shirt as he stared over his shoulder at Laney's house, so perfect and neat.

What the hell was he doing? Was he going to run away, too?

He needed answers and he needed them now.

Austin strode to the front door and lifted his hand to knock, but quickly decided against it. He tried the doorknob. It turned easily and the door opened.

"Unlocked again," he muttered. Not locking doors may be normal practice in Granger, but he still didn't like it. Somehow he had to convince Laney to be more careful.

Austin peeked inside, hoping to see Laney there waiting for him in the living room, but it was deserted.

He walked in, closed and locked the door. For some odd reason, before Laney had ever invited him inside, he'd imagined her home would be decked out in red-and-white-checked curtains and other country kitsch, to go along with Granger's small-town vibe.

On the contrary, the furnishings were contemporary and sophisticated, just like her, and would be perfectly in style in almost all of the cities he often visited on business and for pleasure.

However, with the large-screen television mounted on the wall and a sexy woman like Laney snuggled up in his arms, he knew it would be easy to put his feet up and start feeling very comfortable. Almost as if he was home, and that was a dangerous sign.

Ignoring the urge to turn on the television to check the latest scores on ESPN, Austin made his way down a short hallway toward the kitchen, but discovered Laney wasn't there, either.

He was locking the kitchen door when suddenly his ears picked up the sound of water running through pipes. He stared at the ceiling. Although he'd never been on the second level of Laney's home, that minor detail wasn't going to stop him now. He started up the stairs, his heart pounding in his chest. It was time that he got answers to all his questions, and that he and Laney settled things once and for all.

There were several rooms extending down the hallway, however only one door was closed. He put his hand on the knob, but decided against barging right in.

A short time later he heard the water shut off and he knocked on the door.

"Laney. It's me. We need to talk."

She opened the door, wearing a short white terry-cotton robe, and he drew in his breath as his eyes flitted down her body. Water still glistened on her skin and her nipples puckered against the thin fabric. He hardened immediately, suddenly aware of how difficult it would always be to tamp down his desire for Laney, whether he was angry with her or not.

If she was surprised to see him, she hid it well. Still he saw her upper lip tremble just a bit, as she held on to the door.

"I told you there's nothing more to talk about," she said softly. Her voice had a glimmer of expectation.

His hope for a resolution grew stronger when she didn't slam the door in his face. Instead, she turned on her bare feet and he watched her drift slowly across the carpeted floor, her bare legs flashing and teasing him to distraction in her short robe, and he followed.

Laney sat down on a tufted stool at her dressing table and began to brush her hair in long, even strokes. She stared straight ahead into the mirror, as if she were trying to ignore him.

Austin stood behind, just inches away from her right shoulder. His erection strained boldly in his dark denim jeans, craving the warmth that emanated from her still damp skin, hidden under cotton.

He took a deep breath and thought he saw her eyes dart toward his torso, or at least near the location of his hips. Blood rushed to his core, tightened and lengthened, his body betraying his attempt at restraint. Couldn't she see what she was doing to him? he wondered. Just one turn of her head and she'd be...

Seconds later, her eyes settled back in their original position. Staring ahead, brushing away, stirring his lust and driving him crazy.

"I'm struggling to believe you, Laney, and I really want to understand." He paused and swallowed, struggling to control his physical need for her. "It would help me a great deal if you would tell me why it took you so long to tell me about the baby," he said quietly.

Her hand stopped in midair and she looked down at her lap, the hairbrush now clasped in her palms.

She heaved a deep sigh. "Because we'd only been together one night and I was afraid that you wouldn't think it was yours." She looked up, her eyes flashing. "And that's exactly what happened, isn't it?"

Austin closed his eyes a moment against her accusing stare and the memories unwittingly came flooding back. The stark truth was that he'd lost valuable time with Laney because he'd been fooled in the past.

"You're right," he confessed, opening his eyes. "A long time ago, another woman I'd had a brief relationship with had claimed to be pregnant and that the child was mine, and it turned out not to be true. All she wanted was to extort money from me." He took a shuddering breath. "I knew you didn't want money, but I was stupid and I initially lumped you into the same category as her, even though I knew deep down that it was wrong. I'm truly sorry. Will you ever forgive me?"

Laney didn't turn; instead she peered at his reflection in the mirror, and her face wore a hesitant smile.

"It would be easier to forgive you if you forgave me, too," she whispered.

Austin placed his hands on her shoulders. They felt small, but strong underneath his palms. "I already have, Laney. I forgave you on the day you gave me the sonogram of our child. I knew that you had accepted me as the father of our baby."

Slowly, he bent forward slightly and moved his hands down her arms, until his cheek was next to hers. He stared at their reflection in the mirror, and he felt like a king. She was so beautiful and the desire to kiss her was so strong that he reached for her brush to distract himself.

He stood and when he began to brush, he watched her eyes flutter closed, a tiny smile of pleasure on her lips. Her thick hair felt so soft flowing through his fingers and he bit the inside of his mouth as his erection began to pulse more urgently.

Moments later, he gave in to his urges and swept the hair away from her neck with one hand. Without warning, he bent and softly kissed the skin behind the crest of her ear.

"But, Laney, I still don't know if you will accept me." He mouthed low, watching the mirror closely for her reaction.

Her mouth pursed deliciously as he placed his fingers in her hair and massaged her scalp. At the same time, his tongue traced the soft flesh of earlobe over and over again. She begin to writhe in her seat and Austin saw that the tie that held her robe together was beginning to loosen, and some of the fabric had inched up her thigh.

He moved to her other earlobe, took it into his mouth and sucked, enjoying the sweet moan from the woman he loved.

The woman he loved.

The thought took him by surprise, but he knew it was true. He also knew he wasn't ready to utter the words. Right now, he only wanted to show her.

The robe loosened even more, revealing Laney's rounded abdomen and the dark nest of curly hair beneath that hid his favorite place to lick and explore.

Her eyes met his in the mirror, and Austin expected her to tighten the sash. Instead she allowed her robe to slip from her shoulders and fall to the floor, her eyes taunting him to look and desire her body.

His mouth went dry and the hair on his arms tingled at the sight of her in the mirror. The area around her nipples seemed larger and darker than he remembered, and he had to mentally restrain himself from reaching out and grabbing her breasts.

Suddenly, Laney swiveled around in her seat and, without a word, laid her head against the front of his jeans and began to roll her soft cheek against the expanse of his hard length.

Austin weaved his hands into her hair as she tugged his shirt from his waistband, then began to unbutton it slowly. Too slowly for him, and he quickly finished the rest and tossed his shirt on the floor.

The air felt cool on his skin, but Laney's fingers felt like fire as she traced the muscles of his abdomen, while licking around and in his bellybutton.

She undid his jeans and his thigh muscles twitched in anticipation as she slowly eased them down, followed by his underwear. He swift-kicked both articles of clothing aside and his hips involuntarily thrust forward toward her mouth.

When she turned toward him, grasped and began to noisily suck, his mind went completely blank and all he could do was feel.

Her hair strung between his fingers, the exquisite pull of her lips and the greedy swirl of her tongue on his penis, the feel of her soft hands clutching his tightened buttocks.

His breaths were short. Hitched here and there with the deep groans of a man completely controlled by a woman, as she took him into herself deeper and deeper.

It was like she was trying to possess him and it was working. Austin was completely under her tortuous spell. But he didn't want their lovemaking to end so quickly.

"Oh, God, Laney." He drew away reluctantly and caught her face in his palms as they separated. He watched, completely mesmerized as she spread her legs, until she was straddling the stool. His body shook from intense need as he stroked her cheek over and over again with one thumb.

Unable to resist any longer, Austin reached down and felt Laney's breasts, his mouth watering at the feel of her large, tight nipples.

"I'm not leaving you. Not ever," he muttered thickly.

He gently squeezed one nipple and she abruptly stood up, nearly knocking him from his feet, and he feared he had hurt her somehow.

But when she faced the mirror and looked at their reflection, he was relieved to see that her eyes were filled with desire.

"Then stay with me tonight," she whispered, drawing his arms loosely around her waist.

Austin drew in a sharp breath as she hastily pushed the stool away with her foot, bent and leaned her elbows on the dressing table. He dropped his arms from her waist in surprise and his eyes widened at the sight of her round ass. It seemed to glow and beckon him as he moved slowly toward her. His penis sprang forth painfully and when he made sudden contact with her flesh, she moaned.

He wanted just to drive himself into her right now, but he had to make sure she wanted him to. She was pregnant with his child. He didn't want to hurt her and was willing to sacrifice his own pleasure to keep her and their baby safe.

Still, she wasn't making it easy for him.

He swallowed hard and blurted, "Are you sure?"

Laney turned around, wrapped her arms tightly around his neck and nodded. "Completely."

"But what about the baby?" he muttered stupidly, not sure if he would somehow harm their child by making love. "Won't it hurt?"

She shook her head and leaned it against his shoulder. "I'll let you know if anything is wrong. Right now, all I want you to do is kiss me."

He pressed against her and she lifted her head. When his lips found hers it seemed as though his world had just begun. Her tongue dipped into his mouth as she swayed against him, and he opened one eye to watch himself in the mirror as he cupped his hands around the lower curve of her buttocks.

Austin broke away, grabbed her hips and spun her around, and she bent at the waist, balancing her weight on the dressing table with her palms. He licked his lips and watched in the mirror as her breasts hung in the air, her hardened nipples pointing down like blunt daggers.

He stepped forward, reached one hand around her waist and then angled down through the dark mass of tight yet soft curls. Laney's head dropped forward and she panted while he explored her folds, so vibrant and wet, with his fingers. She was ready, and so was he.

Austin drew his hand back, but she caught it and licked her wetness from his fingers, so slowly that he thought he would come without even being inside her. He groaned and pulled his hand away and placed it on the small of her back, gently pushing her down, until her body was parallel with the dressing table.

Laney braced her hands on the surface and stared at him in the mirror. He stood stock-still, rooted in place by her sensuality, as he watched her eyes glaze over with desire. She was no longer a fantasy.

Every beautiful sight he'd ever seen could never compare to seeing Laney, her eyes wide, mouth slightly open and her ass tilted up, waiting for him with a wicked half smile.

"If you don't make love to me right now, I'll scream," she said breathlessly.

He positioned himself behind her, reached out and placed one hand on her waist as he clasped the other hand around his thick penis.

"How about I make you scream anyway?"

She bit her lip in response and her eyes slid shut as he ran a finger down the cleft of her buttocks and slowly guided himself into her.

At the first contact, Austin gritted his teeth as her inside muscles clenched him firmly, so warm and insistent. He grabbed her hips, planted both feet firmly on the floor and began to slip inside and out. Slowly. Cautiously.

But soon, Austin was caught up in the raw sound of her moaning and the sight of her breasts keeping time with the slick-slap of their coupling. The erotic vision in front of him, Laney's mouth open and, at times, her head rolling from side to side in ecstasy, was almost too much for him to handle.

He closed his eyes, gripped her hips tighter and steadily picked up his pace, not drawing out of her body as much, staying close, yet pumping hard, his entire being homed in on bringing them both to that invisible point of no return.

He opened his eyes to meet hers and they openly watched each other in the mirror. In the reflection was seared the sensual, desperate and unforgettable clamor of mutual release.

Hours later, Laney awoke in semidarkness. Austin lay on his stomach asleep beside her, his arm cradling her lazily just below her breasts. She traced a circle around his bent elbow with her fingertip, remembering the intimacy of his touch and the passion of their lovemaking. She could never have imagined it would have been better than New Year's Eve, but it was, and she knew that the longer she was with him, the more pleasurable sex would be.

As she watched him sleeping, tears leaked from her eyes, a delayed response, but one she knew couldn't be helped. There was no doubt about it now—she was in love. Not just because he was great in bed, but because he was everything she'd ever wanted in a man. He was masculine and gentle and powerful all at the same time.

But did he feel the same way about her?

She wiped her tears away, turned her head and stared out the windows.

In the distance, she could see the mountains. Snow-capped and majestic, they seemed to buttress the blue-black sky that was infused with streaks of orange and pink. The sun was setting, but to Laney, it felt like a brand-new day.

She turned back and gazed at Austin. He was a beautiful man, a good man, and she knew he would be a wonderful father. Her heart swelled and she knew that her deepest wish was that maybe one day they would be a family.

"I could wake up next to you every day," she whispered.

A few second later, she felt a series of kisses on her rib cage and hitched in a breath.

"Then you'd have to get used to this," Austin said thickly.

He lifted his body up slightly on his right elbow and moved his lips from her rib cage to the swell of her left breast. She closed her eyes as he rolled her sideways to face him.

"Think you could handle it?"

When she opened her eyes, his lips hovered just above hers. The hint of a beard covered his jaw.

She nodded. "Keep kissing me like that and I can conquer the world."

Austin regarded her through half-lidded eyes. "I don't doubt it. You've already conquered my heart."

Laney gasped and she put her hand on his chest. "Do you really mean that?"

He clasped her hand next to his heart. "Laney, I've been attracted to you from the very beginning."

Her eyes fluttered open and she felt a pleasure shiver in her belly. "You never said anything to me. In fact, you barely said anything at all."

He shrugged. "What can I say? I'm shy," he replied with a half grin.

His deep voice resonated through her body and she tore her hand away from his.

"You? Shy?" She slapped him on his shoulder playfully. "I don't believe it."

"Remember when I came to town a year or so ago and met with your mother? Can I tell you a secret?" At her eager nod, he continued. "I liked you then."

She giggled. "And here I thought you only wanted to buy one of my mother's horses."

"And I did. That was one of the most expensive purchases I've ever made. But at least I got a chance to see you. Briefly."

"I was in training," she huffed pleasantly. "Can you blame me for not sticking around for a long conversation?"

He kissed her hand. "No. Not at all. And I had to forgive you for snubbing me in London when I saw you with that gold medal around your beautiful neck on television."

She shivered as he drew one finger into his mouth and sucked. "I sent you a thank-you note for the roses. Even though I had to give them to one of my teammates."

Her finger popped out of his mouth. "At the time, I didn't know you were allergic."

"You know now."

He nodded and pulled her close to him. "I know a lot about you now. But I'd like to know more."

She kissed him on the nose. "I want to know more about you, too, Austin. The baby is—"

"—a wonderful miracle," Austin interrupted. "But even if he, or she, hadn't happened, I still wanted to be with you. I just hadn't figured out how to get your attention off your horses and on me."

Austin grew quiet and pensive. He ran his thumb across her chin and she shivered with delight. "No matter what happens, let's always remember how we got here."

His serious tone made grateful tears spring to her eyes and yet, as he slowly started to make love to her again, she couldn't help but be afraid that their feelings were as fragile as the life she held within her.

Chapter 8

"I'm having an attack of déjà vu," Laney said, as she wrenched the seat belt over her body and buckled herself in.

She looked over at her home, where she and Austin had spent most of the weekend in bed, and sighed. He'd proven himself again and again to be a sensitive and urgent lover, and a part of her wished they didn't have to leave.

She turned back to Austin, who was putting on his own seat belt.

"I've already had my checkup and my next appointment isn't until a few weeks from now," she protested.

"This is just a precaution," Austin reassured her.

"But I'm fine," she insisted. "Just because all of a sudden I have two left feet, that doesn't merit an emergency trip to the doctor."

Austin put the key into the ignition and started the car, his mouth set in a firm line.

He turned to her. "You tripped and almost fell twice in the house in the past twenty-four hours. I think we should get you checked out. Just to make sure that the baby is okay."

"But my new doctor said he was booked, remember?

If I wasn't Laney Broward, gold medalist, I don't think I would have even been able to get an appointment with him, even with a referral. The man is that busy."

Austin gunned the engine and shifted the vehicle in Reverse, and then turned it around. "We're not going to see him. We're going to see a new doctor in Granger. And don't worry, I made sure she has admitting privileges to the hospital in Helena, just in case."

Laney raised a brow. "'She'?"

"Dr. Jenna Taylor, a family-practice physician whose father is a client of mine back in Dallas. I'm not sure when she arrived in town, but she had an appointment and that's all that matters to me."

He eased the Land Rover onto the dirt road, which was empty of trucks, tractors and roadkill, and headed west into town.

Austin put his hand on her thigh. "I know you think I'm being overprotective here, but I just want you and the baby to be safe."

Laney leaned over and kissed him on the cheek. "I know and I'm grateful for it." She snuggled back against the seat and sighed. "I guess I'm going to have to get used to this kind of treatment."

Austin grinned. "In the words of the former governor of Alaska, 'You betcha!'"

Laney burst out laughing. "You know, I can't wait to introduce you to Brooke, my brother's new wife. Sometimes she's as corny as you are!"

He flashed her a hurt look. "Trying to get rid of me already?"

She smiled and shook her head. "Never. You're stuck with me, and she's totally in love with Jameson."

"That's a good thing," he answered and she wondered idly if he'd ever thought about marriage. Instead of asking him, she turned and admired the scenery flowing outside her window.

"Have you ever thought about leaving here?"

Laney shifted in her seat and gave him a horrified look. "Granger? No way. It's my home."

"But don't you ever get bored?"

"Only when there's no work to do. For a Broward, that's never. Sometimes it's hard for me to just relax." She leaned her head back. "Ever since my brothers and I were little, my father drummed into our heads the value of a hard day's work. Jameson and I took to the ranching lifestyle like moths around a light, but Wes? Not so much. He actually sold his part of the homestead to Samara Lionne!"

Laney was surprised and pleased when Austin made a face. "I bet your dad didn't approve of that," he commented.

She shook her head. "No way. He's extremely driven and he sacrificed a lot to raise heritage cattle and build the BWB to what it is today. He's taught all of us to do the same in our own endeavors, but I know he was hurt when Wes turned his back on ranching."

Austin frowned. "What's Wes going to do now?"

She shrugged. "No one knows. He and his fiancée, Lydia, are traveling. Not many people know this, but she is, or rather was, Samara Lionne's personal assistant."

Austin arched a brow. "Really? What happened?"

She dropped her voice a notch. "When Samara heard that Lydia was quitting her job to be with Wes, some people said her scream was louder than a coyote's howl."

Austin laughed. "Do you really believe that?"

She shook her head. "I don't know what to believe about Samara. Nobody does, least of all my family. Everyone thinks that's why she's having this ball. To appeal to the good sense of the Browards and for the community."

"Sounds to me like Samara's trying to get in good with your father and mother," Austin alleged.

Laney nodded in agreement. "But there are a lot of people in Granger who wish she would just get out of town."

Austin dropped Laney off at the doctor's office, parked his truck and strolled into the local drugstore. He paid for his purchases in cash and was walking out when he spotted the local newspaper. He picked up it and read the headline.

Oh, God, he thought. *Laney.*

He stuffed the brown paper bag with his purchases under his arm and scooped up all the newspapers, knowing it wouldn't do much good, but he had to do something. He turned back to the cashier, who was with another customer, and tossed a bill on the countertop.

Austin was already halfway out the door when he heard the young woman cry out, "Sir! We don't take one-hundred-dollar bills here."

He ignored her and kept walking toward his car, only stopping to dump the pile of newspapers into a trash can.

All but one.

When Laney walked out of the doctor's office, Austin was there leaning against his truck, frowning.

Her heart sank. "What's wrong?"

He shook his head. "You first. What did the doctor say?"

"Everything's fine. The baby's fine. Now why don't you tell me why you look like your prized horse just lost a race?"

Austin pushed himself away from the truck and he twisted his head to the left and the right, looking down both sides of the street.

She followed his glance, saw nothing of importance, but felt a faint tremor down her spine.

Then he gestured toward her with one arm, as if he wanted to protect her from something. She went to him and he put his arm around her, pulling her close.

"I have something to show you, but you have to promise me that you won't overreact, and most of all, that you won't blame me."

Laney shrank away from his touch, scared by the serious tone in his voice. "I won't promise anything blind, without any information to go on," she said, trying to keep calm. "What is it that you need to show me?"

"Wait here," he instructed.

She watched as he circled around her to the driver's side, opened the door and quickly slammed it shut.

He pivoted back and handed her the newspaper.

She read the headline and she felt the blood drain from her face.

TARNISHED GOLD?

Laney Broward, the famed horse breeder and member of the U.S. Equestrian Team, may have won her gold medal as a result of efforts not thoroughly her own.

Sources allege that Austin Johns, a Broward family friend and the man purported to be the father of her unborn child, may have had undue influence in her win.

A potential investigation into the allegations is currently being evaluated, which could result in Ms. Broward being stripped of her gold medal.

"Laney Broward felt it necessary to hide the fact that she was pregnant. It's clear she can't be trusted," said a Granger resident, who spoke to a reporter on condition of anonymity.

Johns, who is a world-renowned horse breeder and owner of The Perfect Shot, one of the most successful and lucrative thoroughbred racehorses in the country, has been spotted in Granger over the past several weeks. He is rumored to be renting a home in the area as he awaits the birth of Laney Broward's child. Phone calls to his Dallas home yesterday were not returned.

The article was accompanied by a picture of Laney, one of Austin and a red question mark in the middle of them.

The nightmare is starting all over again, she thought, willing herself not to cry. "Where did you get this?" she demanded.

He pointed to the left. "At Fitz drugstore, right down the street.

She moaned, folded the newspaper and handed it to him.

He tucked it under his arm again. "I immediately

bought all the copies that were leftover and, except for this one, dumped them all in the trash. I don't know how many more were bought this morning, though."

Now she knew.

So this was the reason for the funeral hush when she'd walked into the waiting room, the sidelong glances and the whispering that started immediately after the nurse had called her for her appointment.

"When will this end?" she cried out in frustration and to no one in particular. "Why is somebody trying to persecute me?"

Her success was the result of years of training, hard work and sacrifice. She'd put the sport she'd loved since she was a child ahead of everything, including her family and even her romantic life. To think that someone would allege that her gold medal win was a complete sham was almost beyond her comprehension.

Laney was so upset by the article that it felt like the blood in her veins seared hot through her body, yet she shivered uncontrollably with hurt and anger.

Austin put both hands on her shoulders and tried to hold her. "Don't let it upset you."

She wrenched away from his embrace and took a step away. "What are you talking about? My entire name is being smeared like a cow patty on the bottom of somebody's shoe, and you tell me not to be upset."

She was nearly shouting now. A mother and her young son, both of whom had the wide-eyed look of tourists, stared at her while passing by on the adjacent sidewalk. Laney gave the woman a hard stare and they quickly hurried away.

Austin noticed and said, "Why don't we get in the car and talk about this on the drive home?"

At first, Laney stood her ground and refused to get into the car. She was tired of running, tired of hiding and more than that, tired of what she deemed was an invasion of her privacy. But after a few minutes, she nodded reluctantly.

However, when Austin tried to open the door for her, she pushed his hand away. "I got it," she muttered, tugging it open herself.

She waited until Austin was behind the wheel and pulling out of the parking space before asking, "Is it true? Did you talk to the judges? Pay them off?"

He glanced over, a hurt look in his eyes. "I can't believe you're even asking me that question."

"Why were you in London anyway?" she asked, not bothering to hide the suspicion she felt in her voice. "You had no business there, none of your horses were in the events."

Austin made a left turn and glanced over at her. "What…so now you're telling me that because of a stupid article that I'm not allowed to go to London?"

She ignored his comment. "Just tell me why you were there, Austin. The real reason."

"To see if London Bridge was really falling down," he quipped. "Why do you think I was there?"

"Ha-ha, very funny," she snapped. "I don't know, Austin. That's what I'm trying to find out."

They were out of downtown Granger and back on the country road that led to Laney's home. Suddenly there was the harsh sound of tires crunching gravel as Austin pulled the truck over on the side of the road.

"What are you doing?" she asked, looking around. "Why are you stopping the car?"

Austin braked, leaned forward and draped his arms over the steering wheel.

"Trying to get you to see what's right in front of you."

She stared out the front window, perplexed and angry, his words barely a ripple in her mind. All she could see were the headlines blaring, the townsfolk of Granger whispering and her reputation being trampled to death.

All because of one man.

A man who she thought cared about her deeply.

The threat of being stripped of her medal wasn't the worst part, although that would hurt her deeply. Nor was the fact that she probably wouldn't ever be able to compete in any equestrian event ever again, amateur or professional. As a new mom, it would probably be a while before she felt up to competing again anyway.

What bothered her the most was that her reputation, and that of the Broward family, was hanging in the balance.

What scared her the most was that someone out there, perhaps that "anonymous Granger resident," was watching her every move.

How else could they have known that Austin was in town, let alone the fact that he was the father of her baby? She'd only told her family. It was nobody else's business.

"Laney, listen to me, please. I had nothing to do with this article, nor did I have anything to do with influencing anyone. The whole idea is ludicrous. You have to believe me."

She turned to Austin, and her eyes didn't see the man who had made love to her so passionately. They only saw a man who seemed bent on hurting her.

"I don't know what to believe anymore. Just take me home," she said curtly.

"Do you mean to tell me after all we've been through, especially in the past forty-eight hours, that you would throw that all away because of one stupid article?"

Laney sighed, and a part of her knew that he had a point. But she couldn't take the risk. Not anymore. "I'm not throwing anything away. I'm just trying to be careful. I need time to investigate these allegations and until I find out the truth, we should probably stay away from each other."

"Stay away from you? How can I do that when I—" Austin laid his forehead on the steering wheel. "God, I care about you so much, can't you see that?"

All Laney wanted to see was the backside of his truck, driving far away from her.

"Take me home, Austin."

Without another word, he slammed the vehicle in gear and drove. When he reached her house, she had a little trouble unbuckling her seat belt, so that when she finally did, Austin was already out and had opened the passenger-side door.

He offered her his hand, but she alighted without his help and made her way to the front porch.

She opened the door, and was about to close it in his face when he stopped it with his hand.

"Don't do this, Laney."

Tears made her eyes smart, yet she held them back, not wanting him to see how much she wished things between them could be different.

"Go home, Austin. I promise I won't fight you on joint custody." Her voice broke, but somehow she pushed through the pain. "Just go home to Dallas, where you belong."

She closed the door, and for the first time in a long time, she locked it. Too bad she hadn't done the same with her heart.

Chapter 9

This is crazy, Austin thought as he braked his Land Rover to a stop. On his way up the private road to the BWB Ranch, he had counted ten stables, but he knew there were probably more. The Browards were among the largest landowners in the state of Montana. The massive structures were hundreds of feet long and housed the family's heritage cattle and prized thoroughbreds.

He stared at the stable directly in front of him, trying to quell the butterflies in his stomach. It was so unlike him to be nervous, and yet here he was, hoping that the prettiest member of the Broward family hadn't spotted him on her family's land, and that its most powerful member wouldn't shoot him on the spot.

"The old man probably won't even talk to me," Austin muttered under his breath. "Like father, like daughter."

As soon as the words were out of his mouth, he felt shame wash over him. Laney may have her reasons for not speaking to him; he didn't understand them, but he knew he had to respect her decision. But that didn't mean he had to like it or accept it.

No way was he going to accept it.

Several days had passed since he and Laney had last spoken on her doorstep, where she'd practically ordered him to go back to Dallas. That was like telling him to crawl back to his past, where he was a rich, albeit lonely, child.

Now he was a rich man who, although he would never admit to anyone that he was lonely, would admit to one thing: he was in love with Laney Broward.

Austin took a deep breath, stepped out of the car and adjusted his Stetson.

Now he needed the help of her father to make Laney see what he already knew.

She was a woman he would call his own.

She was his future.

Steven Broward was a patient man. It was a skill that had been passed down through generations.

In troubled economic times, his grandfather Silas and later on, his father, Charles, had built up the BWB Ranch one horse at a time. Now Steven continued the tradition of slow, steady growth through the breeding of heritage cattle and other farm animals.

Growth that was now threatened by outsiders buying up the land around Granger.

City dwellers, he thought, wrinkling his nose, who now had it in their craw to be ranchers. He'd heard talk about plans to build McMansions with three-car garages and stables populated with horses purchased off the internet.

The internet! Steven thought with a disgusted sigh. It was just as well because the mountains would have to split in two before he'd sell any of his horses to them. He might as well sell his soul to the devil.

All of this was happening because Samara Lionne had established a home here by purchasing Wes's land.

His son had sold his homestead and now one of his neighbors was a woman who regularly graced the tabloids Gwen liked to read. There was a rumor floating around that she was going to turn her new "home" into a movie set.

"Gah," he muttered under his breath. "I hate Hollywood."

While all the gawkers, tourists and new residents had initially been great for his business, he knew it was short-lived. They were like bees attracted to an open can of soda on a hot day. The glamorous fizz bubbling over the top lured them in, until they took a dive and drowned in syrupy sweetness.

Annoying as they were, right now Samara Lionne and the out-of-towners were the least of his problems.

Steven folded his hands on his metal desk, which was battered from years of use, and waited for the man who had impregnated his daughter. And who might be responsible for her possibly losing her gold medal. And who was the subject of many a late-night argument recently with his wife, Gwen.

From his office window, which was located in the very first stable on his property, he'd seen Austin Johns approach in his truck, the value of which would have bought several hundred pounds of feed for his cattle.

Not that he judged how Austin spent his obvious wealth. After all, although Steven drove a truck that was more than thirty years old, even he was partial to the occasional Cuban cigar.

No, he judged Austin merely on the value he had to the Broward family. And right now, with all the trouble he was causing, Austin Johns, much like Samara Lionne, was an extreme liability.

Several minutes later Steven heard a car door slam and footsteps crunching gravel. He quickly busied himself with a pile of paperwork that seemed to have an uncanny ability to repopulate.

Austin knocked on the doorjamb. Steven had never installed a door in his office, preferring to allow his employees and the occasional wayward cow to have easy access to him. The earthy stench of the stables didn't bother him, rather it was a reminder of all he'd accomplished and all that he still needed to do.

"Mr. Broward, can I see you for a minute?"

Steven stared at the handsome man in front of him. Had he ever been that young? Tall and lean, Austin had the type of barely-restrained energy that, depending how it was utilized, attracted either trouble or admiration.

He looked at his watch, an old Timex that had been repaired about as many times as his '79 Chevy.

"Okay, but I got a feeling this is going to take more than a minute," he said, pointing to a chair in the corner. "Have a seat."

Austin sat with his back straight, like he was awaiting judgement from the principal, and it made Steven wonder what he was hiding.

He put his pen down on the stack of paper. "What's going on?"

"It's about Laney and—" he faltered.

"Are you going to ask for her hand in marriage?"

Austin knit his brows together, and Steven almost laughed at the look of shocked surprise on his face.

"With all due respect, sir, do people even do that anymore?"

Steven pondered the question a moment. His own marriage to Gwendolyn had been arranged over thirty-four years ago. Despite all the chatter around town that it wouldn't last, it had. His marriage to Gwen was strong, stable and loving.

He shrugged. "Thought you might want to revive an old tradition, especially since you already got my daughter pregnant."

Austin forced a smile. "It's hard to think about marriage when the woman you care about won't even see you. I was hoping you could help."

Steven eased out of his chair and walked over to the glass window that overlooked an open area of the stable.

"I've tried everything," Austin continued.

He glanced back. "Roses?" At Austin's nod, he said, "She's allergic to them."

"I found that out, so I bought her daisies and I—"

Steven waved his hand, not wanting to hear the angst in Austin's voice. Something about it reminded him of himself as a young man. He preferred not to think of the past, about things he could never change.

He leaned one shoulder against the glass. "Laney's always been headstrong, like her mama. Like the fiery stallions they both breed. I'm afraid I can't be much help to you. Neither can the latest headline."

Austin leaned forward in his chair. "I didn't have anything to do with that. She won that medal on her own talent and merit. You have to believe me!"

Clearly, Austin wanted some sort of redemption, for his guilt to be lifted. But Steven wasn't ready to give it to him yet, if ever.

By way of habit, his eyes momentarily swept the interior of the stable, looking for anything out of place, but there was nothing, a testament to the strong grip he kept on the ranch.

"Over the past few days," said Steven, "I've asked myself, 'How could all of this happen to Laney?' and 'Why?'"

"Come up with any answers yet?"

Steven turned again toward Austin. "Only that someone in this town seems to have a grudge against my family, and they're using you and Laney as pawns."

Austin sat back, a look of disbelief on his face. "Who would do that?"

"I don't know. But I also don't need any more fodder for the rumor mill," Steven replied sternly.

"Are you asking me to stay away from Laney?" Austin demanded.

He linked his hands behind his back. "You're a grown man. Draw your own conclusions."

Austin shook his head. "I'm sorry, but I can't do that, Mr. Broward."

"Because she's carrying your child," he concluded, internally pleased at Austin's comment.

Austin took his Stetson off and idly rubbed his hand over his head. "At first, that was the only reason," he admitted. "But now…"

"You're in love with her."

Austin stared at him wide-eyed before nodding. "Yes."

Steven regarded the man who'd given him his first grandchild. There wasn't another gift more precious than that, and he smiled wanly. "I know better than to stand in the way of two lovebirds."

Austin arched a brow. "Two? What do you know that you're not telling me?"

He crossed his arms. "Only that when you find love,

even in the worst or most impossible of circumstances, don't let it go."

Austin grinned. "It sounds like you're talking from experience."

Steven noted a youthful curiosity in his voice, and he was almost tempted to share a story from his past, but quickly decided against it.

He shrugged. "I might be."

Austin tipped his hat back and got up to leave. "Thanks for the advice, and I'm sorry for all the trouble and worry that I've caused you, your wife and the whole Broward family."

Steven waved his apology aside. "A lot of sleepless nights, for sure, but we're all up at the crack of dawn anyway. Gwen and I hope that you two work things out, for the sake of our grandchild."

Austin nodded, and was almost out of the room when he turned and he leaned against the doorjamb. His stance was a lot more relaxed than when he'd first come in.

"If I did come to you and ask for Laney's hand in marriage, what would you say?"

The question jarred Steven, for he knew all too well how fleeting love could be. He wanted all of his children to be happy. His sons, Wes and Jameson, had found love by way of the most unexpected events, and their lives now seemed blissful.

Could the same thing happen for Laney with Austin? Under the current circumstances, he highly doubted it. There was too much bad publicity and uncertainty. Plus, Steve knew that Austin was a jet-setter, and he feared that if they married, Laney would shun the ranch, just like Wes did. Maybe she would even sell her homestead to Samara.

She was his only daughter. He couldn't lose her!

Life was a relentless gamble. Just when you thought you'd had it whipped, it turned around and laughed. And sometimes you had to laugh with it.

But no man was going to gamble with his daughter's heart.

Finally, Steven shook his head no, ignoring the shock and disappointment on Austin's face before he strode off without another word.

Steven waited until he heard the sound of the engine before he walked outside. His refusal of Austin's request wasn't so much a denial as it was a challenge. If Austin truly did love Laney, now was his chance to prove it—to the entire Broward family.

Chapter 10

Laney cuddled under her blanket and curled even deeper into the plush sofa in her living room.

Tomorrow night was the Granger Ball and she would be a no-show. One look in the dressing room mirror that morning while shopping for maternity clothes had clinched an already sound decision.

Although her mother and her friends would take one look at her and disagree, the truth was that she felt fat, dumpy and wholly unattractive.

"To hell with Samara Lionne," she muttered, grabbing the remote.

She stuck her bottom lip out like a pouty child as she flipped through the channels, only because there was no one around to see her do it.

She was going to spend the rest of the day and all of the next as a cranky couch potato. Thought-provoking daytime TV, mind-numbing reality shows and a few old Westerns would numb her emotions. Either that or she'd die from boredom.

Laney pulled down the top of her favorite sweatshirt over her growing belly. As she did so, she placed her hand over the child growing beneath. "It's just you and me today," she whispered. "Maybe I'll put on some *Sesame Street,* just to get you used to it."

She, on the other hand, was struggling to get used to being without Austin, whom she hadn't seen since he'd taken her to the doctor several days ago, and she'd practically slammed the door on his face.

Not even a visit with Stella Rose had cheered her up. She had nuzzled at her neck and whinnied, as if she were standing in solidarity with Laney's plight. Or maybe Stella just missed the sugar cubes that Austin had often given her. Just like Laney missed his sweet and stormy kisses.

She'd asked Austin to give her some space, and this time, he'd listened to her. Had he finally returned to Dallas? However, this was one time she wished he hadn't.

It's all so confusing, she thought.

"Woohoo!"

Heart pounding, Laney shot up straight from the couch, turned around and breathed a sigh of relief. It was only Brooke and she was peering through the screen in her front window.

"Hey! What are you doing here?" she called out.

"I texted you that I was stopping by this afternoon. Didn't you get it?"

"Sorry, I turned off my phone when I got home," Laney answered, tossing the blanket aside.

So I won't keep checking for a message from Austin.

"That's okay, but since when do you lock your front door?" her sister-in-law asked through the screen.

Ever since Austin broke in and stole my heart, Laney thought as she got up and padded across the hardwood floor in her bare feet.

She unlocked and opened the door. "I must have done it without thinking." She smirked and gave Brooke a peck on the cheek.

Brooke, holding two huge garment bags, side-stepped her way inside. "It's probably a smart thing to do nowadays. Especially with a lot of new folks in town. Things sure have changed."

"Tell me about it." Laney closed the door. "Those look heavy. Let me help you!"

Brooke twisted away slightly. "I got them." She walked a few more steps and gingerly laid the bundles across the love seat, arranging them carefully so that they would lie smooth. "I can't wait to show you what's inside!"

Laney snuck back to the couch and slipped under the blankets once more.

Brooke turned. "What's wrong?" she asked, eyeing her lumpy shape. "Are you sick?"

Laney wasn't about to go into all the reasons why she felt like bumming around, so she simply replied, "Nope, just trying to catch up on some mindless entertainment."

Brooke turned to the television and lifted a brow. "You're watching *Divorce Court?* Laney, you're not even married!"

"Don't remind me," she said with a scowl, and then forced a hopeful lilt in her voice. "Besides, I can pick up some great tips on what not to do, just in case wedding bells ever ring."

Brooke walked over and sat on the edge of the couch. "Don't worry. It'll happen. Just look at me and Jameson."

"And soon, Lydia and Wes," Laney reminded her. "Two pairs of perfect matches made on the ranch."

"With one perfect pair missing," Brooke added, a glimmer in her eye.

Laney frowned and tapped her head with one finger. "If you're thinking about me and Austin, you've got something missing and it's not us," she grumbled.

"Not missing," Brooke revised. "Simply waiting in the wings for the moment—" she intoned with dramatic flair.

"—when I bop you on the head with this pillow." Laney grabbed one from behind her head. She swung it playfully at Brooke, who promptly ducked out of the way, and Laney ended up hitting herself in the face instead.

The two women doubled over with laughter. By the time they'd calmed down, Laney felt a whole lot better and she was glad for the interruption.

"So show me what's in those bags," Laney said, sitting cross-legged on the sofa.

Brooke unzipped the garment bags and pulled out the dresses.

"They're both so gorgeous!" Laney exclaimed. "Which one will you choose?"

"I'm taking myself out of the equation and letting Jameson have the final decision."

There was something sweet about Brooke's gesture, yet something also curdled in Laney's stomach at the thought of a man having a say in his wife's clothing choices. She knew she was far too independent to allow that to ever happen to her.

"Wow, you're brave. I don't know if I'd let a guy decide my wardrobe."

"He's not deciding what I wear," Brooke retorted,

sounding a bit miffed. "He's choosing what he likes best. Since I love both gowns, I win either way. Get it?"

Laney shook her head and shifted her eyes to the television screen. A couple was face-to-face, arguing. She could almost feel their anger, even though she couldn't hear any words. Relationships were strange. How could anger be so palpable and recognizable, yet love sometimes be so unseen?

Her eyes reached Brooke's. "You're trying to teach me one of the secrets of staying happily married, aren't you?" At Brooke's nod, Laney sighed. "And I've got a lot to learn, don't I?" she asked, a rueful smile on her lips.

Brooke plopped down right next to her, nodding. "And what better people to learn from than your family? I mean, look at your mom and dad. They've been married over thirty years! I've often wondered what's their secret."

"Why don't you ask Gwen?"

Brooke frowned. "I couldn't impose."

Laney clasped her friend's hands. "Why not? My mom loves you."

"I know she does now. I'm lucky she accepted me into the family, after the way Meredith treated Jameson."

Laney shifted against the pillows, looking for a more comfortable spot. "What matters is that you are married to Jameson, not your sister. It would do you good to put all that stuff behind you. It's in the past."

Brooke tossed her curls over her shoulder. "I could give you the same advice, you know."

"It's a different situation with Austin and me."

"Because of the baby?"

Laney nodded. "The baby changes everything."

Brooke was silent for a moment. "No. The baby makes everything possible."

"What do you mean?" Laney asked.

Brooke's hazel eyes darkened. "When I place a blob of clay on my potter's wheel, it's difficult to shape it with only one hand." She paused a moment, as if she were reflecting on something. "Although a baby takes two bodies to create, in a perfect world, it also needs two hands to mold it and two hearts to love it."

In a perfect world, Laney thought. She knew there were millions of single mothers in the U.S. and around the world and that raising a child alone was often thankless and scary. However she often wondered that if they could change their situation and raise their children with help from a stable partner, would they? Was it even worth the risk? At this point in her own life, she wasn't sure.

"I don't know if Austin loves me," Laney finally said.

Brooke smiled patiently. "But if you are blessed to have the father of your child in your life and he's willing to take responsibility, does it really matter at this moment if he loves you, too?"

Laney's eyes slid shut. She knew in her heart that Brooke had a point. The baby's feelings and care had to come first, everything else was secondary.

"No," she whispered.

Brooke patted Laney's hand. "In time, true love will come. Right now, it just happens to be in the shape of your child."

Tears rolled over Laney's cheeks as she looked down and ran one hand over her belly. Brooke was right. The love she sought was right here, nestled within her. She and her baby would be forever tethered, whether Austin was in their lives or not.

Chapter 11

"Are you sure you won't change your mind?" Gwen asked in a wheedling voice. "Everyone will be there."

That's the problem, Laney thought. *Everyone will be there.* Including Austin, whom she suspected would have the entire female population of Granger hanging on his arm immediately upon arrival.

Laney laid her hand across her stomach and reached for a book from the stack she'd brought over to the house. She planned on camping out at the ranch for most of the night, and almost had herself convinced that she wasn't hiding from Austin.

If only she didn't miss him so much.

"I'm sure, Mom. You and Dad go without me, okay? I'll be fine."

She flashed a too-bright smile that Gwen immediately sensed was just for her benefit. Laney may be a world-famous athletic champion, but she was still her little girl and she knew when Laney was upset.

Gwen picked up one of the books. "*Labor Made Easy,*" she read aloud, her eyes widening. "And it's written by a man who is not even a doctor." She clicked her tongue against her teeth. "What does he know about being pregnant?"

Laney mumbled, "I think that one's supposed to be humorous." She quickly opened up her book, a bestselling primer on child-rearing, and hoped that her mother would take the hint. She hesitated telling her to leave her alone, knowing that someday she might be hearing those same words from her own son or daughter.

Gwen put her hands on her hips. "Having a baby is no laughing matter," she said. "It's painful and it's hard work."

Laney considered her mother, who tended to be too serious sometimes, even though she knew she meant well. "Maybe the author has figured out a way to make it funny, too!"

"While he's laughing all the way to the bank, I suppose?"

"I don't know, Mama," she responded with a shrug. "I'm just trying to prepare myself, that's all."

"I know, honey. But your greatest resource for pregnancy information is standing right in front of you," Gwen said, a note of hurt in her voice.

Laney set her book facedown on her lap and reached for her. "Of course, I am going to rely on you. I need you, Mama!"

Gwen sat down next to her daughter and squeezed her hand. "And I'm here for you. No matter what, but—"

"What's wrong?"

Gwen stroked Laney's hair. "I just wish I would have forced you to buy a dress for the ball. Now, if you change your mind, you have nothing to wear."

Laney leaned away from her touch. "I'm not going to change my mind," she insisted. "I want this to be a nice night out for you and Dad. One with no publicity and no cameras."

Gwen chuckled. "Did you forget that the ball is being hosted by Samara? Production trucks from all the major entertainment networks arrived early this morning. It looks like tonight is going to be quite a show."

Even more reason for me to stay home.

Laney cleared her throat. "In that case, until I can get this mix-up sorted out, I should probably lay low anyway."

Gwen pursed her lips. "But I thought you said that when you spoke to your coach, he didn't know anything about the allegations and neither did the committee."

"That's right," Laney nodded. "It appears that the story only broke locally, which is strange, because from the way it was written it had all the hallmarks of a national story. However, there was no mention of it online either, not even TMZ.com."

"Are you saying the story was a fake?"

"Mama. We both know it wasn't true, so of course, it was fake."

Gwen snorted in disgust. "The question is—who planted it and why?"

"I don't know!" she said, unable to keep the frustration out of her voice. The private detective she'd hired had been unable to find out any information, either. The man was completely useless, so she'd fired him that very morning.

"Well, we both know that Austin wouldn't do anything to hurt you." When her daughter remained silent, she reiterated the question. "Don't we, Laney?"

"I don't know, Mama."

She'd gone over and over things again and again in her mind, and she never was able to quite convince herself that Austin hadn't played some role in this latest scandal. Or perhaps somebody he knew didn't want him in Granger, let alone in a relationship with Laney. An old lover, perhaps? Until she knew for sure, she couldn't continue to risk her heart.

"Laney, how could you even think such a horrible thing about Austin?" Gwen said in a shocked voice. "Anyone can see how much he cares for you and the baby."

"I haven't heard from Austin in several days. I don't— I mean, we don't need him," Laney corrected, but she knew the minor slip of her tongue wouldn't fool her mother.

Gwen stood as Laney folded her arms protectively around her belly. "Maybe you don't need him. But did you ever stop to think that maybe he needs you?" She cinched the tie on her robe a little tighter. "I'm going upstairs to get dressed."

Laney watched Gwen walk out of the Great Room. Then she opened up the book and tried to read, but all she could think about was her mother's words.

She slammed the book closed. Austin needing her? That was almost laughable. He was as fiercely independent and ambitious as she was, and yet, Laney knew that he had given up some of his freedom to stay in Granger with her.

Laney stretched out on the couch and yawned. She had no right to be suspicious of his motives, and yet, as she drifted off to sleep, she couldn't help but wonder why he was still hanging around in the area.

Thirty minutes later, Laney's eyes blinked open and she awoke with a start of confusion.

At some point while she was dozing, she'd had the sense that she was no longer alone in the Great Room, but she hadn't the strength or nor the will to wake up.

A dream about Austin had sucked her into the spell of another world. One where they could both live happily without scrutiny or fear. A world she was most happy to stay in—even if it was in her own mind.

Yet it was his cologne that drew her out of her fantasy, a spicy and sensual musk that always reminded her of the passionate kisses they had shared.

She sat up, her elbows sinking into the plush fabric of the L-shaped sofa.

Austin sat at the other end, dressed in a black tuxedo. The broad smile on his face was both charming and mysterious, and it warmed her to the core of her being.

"What are you doing here?" she asked. She was surprised and pleased to see him, and she had to hold herself back from leaping into his arms. "I thought you had gone back to Dallas?"

His smile deepened and his eyes held a mischievous glow. "No way. I told you before I wasn't going to leave you. In fact, I'm here to take you to the Granger Ball."

Her heart did a little flip as he stood and bowed before her. "Me? Why?"

He kissed her hand. "Because you're the prettiest woman in town!" he answered.

Her heart beat faster and while she was flattered, she knew he was mistaken. She felt anything but pretty that evening. "I think you've got the wrong woman," she replied, even though she wanted his words to be true.

She turned her eyes away and gazed down at her outfit. The grey sweatpants, orange fuzzy socks and her favorite thermal T-shirt were not exactly formal wear, but for the moment, they suited her just fine.

Laney closed her eyes and fell back against the pillow, wishing Austin would just go away, while at the same time wishing he would stay.

He didn't answer at first. Instead he gently pulled her up to stand in front of him.

He touched her chin with his fingertip. "No, that's where you're wrong. I've got the right woman."

Before she could say anything, Austin pulled her close. His muscular chest was warm and hard against her cheek. "But I guess she doesn't know it yet. But I'm tonight I'm going to show her just what I mean."

She shivered in his arms as he planted light kisses on her forehead.

Laney stepped away from him to escape the heat that was beginning to flow through her body. "Austin, there's no way I'm going to the ball."

"Why not?"

"I just don't think it's wise for you and me to be seen in public. Not until this story blows over."

Austin frowned. "I told you I had nothing to do with that. It's not true and—"

Laney held up her hand. "I know it's not true, okay?"

"You mean, you finally believe me?"

She nodded. Austin had said he'd never leave her, no matter what, and he hadn't. She didn't know if he loved her, but that fact alone said a lot about his character.

"You stayed right here in Granger, and didn't go off to Dallas, even though I told you to leave. You didn't give up on us, even when I did."

"And I never will," Austin said. But when he moved to kiss her, she put her hand on his chest to stop him.

"What's the problem?"

"I don't want people to think that we're a couple," she blurted out. And yet, deep down, she knew that what she wanted most of all was just the opposite.

Laney watched Austin's face carefully, but there was no outward sign that he was disturbed or hurt by her comment.

Instead, he merely grinned at her, which confused her even more.

"Wait here," he instructed.

She didn't move from where she stood and he was back in moments, hauling three large garment bags over his shoulder. If he hadn't been so tall, the bags would have been trailing on the floor. That's when Laney knew that something was up.

Austin walked down the Great Room steps and carefully draped each garment bag over the back of the sofa.

"What's this?" she asked, watching him unzip the first bag.

"Your golden ticket to the ball," he replied.

Laney gasped at the sight of the elaborate silver gown. The second bag held a red off-the-shoulder one, and the third bag contained a black chiffon that was knee-length.

"Did you buy these?" At his nod, she said, "Thank you. They're all beautiful, but there's no way I'm going to fit into any of them."

"Don't be so sure." Austin folded his arms across his chest. "These are special maternity gowns from the private collection of a New York designer."

"Who?"

"Shh…" said Austin, looking around as if they were

on a secret mission. "If I tell you, the spell will be broken!"

Laney laughed. "What spell?"

"The one that says if you just try one of these gowns on, you're going to fall in love."

"With the gown? Or with you?"

Austin shrugged. "Maybe both!"

They stared at each other for a long moment.

Laney walked to where Austin stood holding all three gowns in his hands, tempting her to reach out and touch them. They were all so beautiful.

"I really shouldn't do this, you know."

"I think you really should." He grinned.

The next thing she knew Austin had draped the garments over her outstretched arm.

"I'll be right back," she said, a wry smile on her face as she quickly headed a short distance down the hall to the powder room, before she changed her mind.

Once inside, she locked the door and hung the dresses on a hook.

The red and black dresses she didn't really care for, as they seemed too plain for her personality and the occasion. But the silver dress was another matter. It was sleeveless, with an intricately woven pattern of silver beads and a modest scoop neck.

Laney quickly tore off her clothes and slipped the dress on. Just as she suspected, it was beautiful and showed off her toned arms to perfection.

But what about her baby bump?

She bit her lip, turned in profile, and smiled in the mirror, pleasantly surprised at how she looked.

The material of the dress was form-fitting, but instead of making her look fat, it made her baby bump look sexy.

Laney took her hair out of the ponytail and fluffed it around her shoulders. All she needed was a little makeup and she'd be ready to go. She wasn't even going to bother trying on the other dresses.

Her heart swelled in her chest. She'd already fallen in love with this one, and with the man who'd purchased it.

She took a deep breath, opened the door and walked back down the hall to the Great Room. As she stood near the stairs, she felt the heat of his dark eyes upon her body.

Austin took her hand and led her down the stairs, and she felt like a queen.

"Wow, you look beautiful. Was I right?" Laney assumed he was talking about the dress. There was no reason to tell him her feelings about him—now or maybe ever.

She nodded. "But I could never accept it."

"You can and you will."

They both turned around to see Gwen walking toward them.

"Mother, how long were you standing there?"

"Long enough to stop you from being a fool." She took her daughter's hand. "Laney, you look beautiful in that gown. There's no reason why you shouldn't accept it, nor is there any reason for you not to attend the ball."

"That's what I've been trying to tell her," Austin interjected. "But she won't listen."

Laney folded her arms. "But what about the media?"

"Darling. I know that, being the baby in the family, you'd like to think that all the attention is going to be focused on you. But the media is not here for you—they're here for Samara."

Laney blushed. "Mama…"

Gwen patted her arm. "If I felt there was any chance of you getting caught up in another scandal tonight, I would stay home with you."

"So you'll come, right?" Austin asked.

Laney bit her lip, trying to think of any other excuse to get out of going to the ball.

She lifted her dress slightly and revealed her bare feet.

"I don't have the proper shoes," she said in a meek voice, wriggling her toes.

"Nice try, darling," Gwen said with a wry grin as she handed Laney her purse. "You can stop by your house on the way to the ball and pick them up."

Laney nodded, trying inwardly to quell her nerves, while Austin dug his car keys out of his pocket, a huge grin on his face.

"Austin, would you mind if I accompanied you both? Steven left early in the limo Samara sent over. He went to pick Wes and Lydia up at the airport, and I'd prefer not to drive alone."

"Absolutely, Mrs. Broward. Samara sent a limo to me as well, but I sent the man on his way. I'll bring the car around."

When he'd gone, Laney and her mother made their way to the foyer.

She slipped into her tennis shoes.

"Mama, I hope I'm not making a mistake."

Gwen pulled her into a hug. "The only way to find out is to attend the ball and see."

Chapter 12

On the drive into town, Laney was lost in her thoughts as she sat in the backseat of Austin's luxurious Mercedes-Benz sedan. Gwen and Austin chattered amiably up front, as if they were old friends.

If Austin ever became a permanent part of the Broward family, Laney knew he would fit right in. Deep down, she was afraid that he wasn't keen on anything that would require him to lay down roots. Business came first, fatherhood would be a distraction and marriage was the ultimate deal killer.

Sure, he was in Granger now, but there'd been no talk about him staying permanently once the baby was born. He also hadn't mentioned anything about joint custody lately, but perhaps he was still working on things with his lawyers. She should be starting the process with her own attorney, but somehow, she hadn't been able to do that yet.

Hope for a real relationship with Austin kept her going and made her happy, despite the turmoil in her life and that of her family, and yet it made her afraid, too.

Her heart sank and Laney stared down at her lap. Still, what was the use of hoping she'd ever be anything to him but the mother of his child?

She smoothed her gown over her protruding belly, enjoying the feel of the beaded fabric as it tickled the palm of her hand, wondering why he'd gone through all the trouble of getting it for her.

Had he done so out of some kind of unspoken obligation? Was that the reason he felt compelled to accompany her to the ball?

Under the cloak of twilight, she lifted her head and stole a glance at Austin. From any vantage point, he was gorgeous, but tonight his presence was laden with mystery.

His magnetism seemed more powerful than ever before, perhaps because her mother was in the car, and she couldn't touch him. She could only inspect him from behind, from the place of a stranger, not as someone who'd been intimate with him.

Laney drew her eyes along his angular jaw, remembering how hard he'd clenched it as she'd traced the gentle curve of his ear with her tongue. She zeroed in on the plump lobe and recalled how his neck had corded when she'd taken it into her mouth and sucked, as she'd stroked her fingers along his close-cut hair.

Finally, her eyes took in the expanse of Austin's broad shoulders. Her hands had barely covered them as she'd clung to him whenever they made love, hanging on the cliff of ecstasy. Afterward, they'd soaked up her tears of fulfillment, strong and welcoming even at rest.

A loud sigh at the pleasurable memories escaped her. Her mother didn't seem to notice, but Austin's eyes caught hers and crinkled in the rearview mirror.

Her gaze snapped down to her lap as she pressed her back against the seat and wished she could just disappear. Thankfully, he didn't turn around, for if he had, he would have seen her blushing like a preacher's virginal daughter.

A few minutes later, they were approaching the hotel when Gwen suddenly exclaimed, "Oh, Lordy, this place is lit up like Times Square."

Laney leaned forward and saw that there were two large spotlights on the roof of The Granger Inn, where the event was being held. She pressed the button for the window and when it was open, she craned her neck outside and saw the searchlights scanning the sky, alerting everyone for miles that something special was happening in Granger.

A myriad of production trucks and news vans lined the road with a rent-a-cop posted near each one. Stretch limos and luxury cars pulled in and out of the hotel entrance, dropping off tuxedoed men and elegantly dressed women.

Throngs of people gawked behind hundreds of feet of red velvet rope, that classic border between the haves and the have-nots, and Laney wondered how many of them wished there were no barriers at all. Her stomach curdled in nervous anticipation. At that moment, she knew she'd trade places with any one of them.

Being in the public eye created a weight of personal responsibility that Laney was only beginning to understand.

She was no longer her own.

Austin pulled the car up to the entrance. "If you ever wanted to walk the red carpet, here's your chance," he quipped.

He got out and handed his keys to the valet.

A uniformed attendant assisted Gwen out of the vehicle, but when he tried to help Laney, Austin brushed him aside.

"I've got her," he said, offering her his hand.

Laney gathered her gown and stepped out of the vehicle.

There was a collective gasp from the crowd and she felt like she was going to faint right there on the red carpet.

Don't let me go, Austin! Please don't let me go!

Although Austin gave no outward sign that he'd heard the reaction of the crowd, he flashed a warm smile and squeezed her hand. She felt a thrill in her veins that quieted her nerves and made her feel protected. Laney knew she had his full support, but did she have his heart?

Austin let go of her hand and bowed slightly.

"Ladies, may I escort you inside?" he asked, offering one arm to Gwen and the other to Laney.

Her mother giggled like a schoolgirl, bent her head and whispered to Laney, "If you don't snatch him up soon, I will!"

With Gwen on Austin's left and Laney on his right, the trio slowly waltzed down the red carpet as the crowd cheered and applauded.

Once they arrived inside, Gwen excused herself to go and find Steven, leaving Austin and Laney alone.

"You were so quiet on the way over here. Are you okay?" he asked.

Laney nodded, inwardly pleased that he'd noticed. "I was just thinking."

"Care to tell me what about?"

She paused a moment, not sure if she should tell him the truth. But now was a good time as any, before they both got caught up in the evening's events.

"I was thinking about second chances and how I'd—"

"Laney!"

They both turned to see Wes and his fiancée, Lydia, approaching them.

She smiled and left Austin's side to hug her big brother.

"Wes, it's so good to see you again," she said.

"The last time I saw you was at the family meeting," Wes remarked. He stepped out of her embrace and took a long look at her.

"How's my little niece or nephew doing?"

"Fine, just fine. Since you left, Mama's been trying to stuff me with her famous cookies, but I've been pretty good."

"I'd say, you look gorgeous. Doesn't she, Lydia?"

Laney hugged her future sister-in-law next.

"She sure does," Lydia affirmed. "You are truly blessed."

"Thank you," Laney replied. "How was Los Angeles?"

"Frivolous, fun and the traffic is a bear, but we love it there, don't we, honey?"

Laney watched as Wes slid a protective arm around Lydia and gazed at her with eyes that were no less than absolutely adoring.

"The smog takes some getting used to, but the weather is phenomenal. Through her connections in the entertainment business, Lydia and I have met some pretty fascinating people."

"Just don't like L.A. too much," Laney warned, brandishing her index finger. "Mom and Dad would probably have a cow if you ever left Granger permanently.

You know how important it is to them to keep the BWB Ranch in the family."

Laney turned and motioned Austin forward, who was waiting patiently in the same spot where she'd left him.

"Wes, you remember Austin, don't you?" she asked.

Austin arrived and extended his hand. "Good to see you again."

"And you, as well," Wes replied and winked. "By the way, good luck!"

Austin looked at Laney and she could see the confusion in his eyes, but all she could do was shrug.

"Umm…thanks?" he stammered. "I think."

Lydia tugged on Wes's arm. "Shh… It's supposed to be a surprise." Wes started to open his mouth, but she grabbed his hand and pulled him away. "We'll catch up with you two later."

When the couple had disappeared into the ballroom, Austin turned to Laney. "What was that about?"

Laney opened her mouth to tell him how it wasn't unusual for her older brother to say things that only made sense to him, but she never got the chance.

For, instead of looking at her, Austin's eyes were on someone else. She turned to see Samara Lionne, flanked by two bodyguards, walking toward them.

She was dressed in a full-length red beaded gown that shimmered and clung to her curves with a deep V-neck that exposed just a hint of her generous cleavage. She had diamonds on her neck, ears and wrists. Laney had no doubt that she wanted a giant rock on her finger, too. By the intensity of her gaze at Austin, she bet Samara wanted him to be the one to put it there.

"Two bodyguards?" Laney whispered, slipping her arm into his. "What does she think is going to happen to her in Granger? Is she afraid of getting pelted with horse manure?"

"Nah, sounds to me like she's already created enough of a stink around here," Austin replied with a straight face.

Laney held back a giggle and whispered back, "I just hope we don't step in it!"

"Mr. Johns, I've been looking all over for you."

Austin bowed. "You've found me."

Samara ignored Laney and ran her hand down Austin's arm. "So I have," she said in a teasing voice. "And I'm hoping that you've heard the good news."

"Not a word. What's up?"

"You and I are both participating in the Cowboy Auction this evening. And I am the Grand Prize!"

"Congratulations," he said. "But you must be mistaken. I am not for sale."

She laughed and it seemed to Laney, who stood and watched, that she was trying her best to charm Austin somehow.

"Darling, neither am I. But all the proceeds are going to charity, so how can you possibly refuse? Besides, I predict you'll be very popular among the ladies." She ran a hand down his arm again and sucked in a breath. "Oh, yes, you're definitely a 'hot item,'" she cooed.

Laney felt her blood begin to boil at the star's overdramatic flirtation. "Cut it out, Samara."

Samara dropped her hand to her side and peered down her nose. "Who are you? Oh, now I remember, the disgraced champion—Laney Broward." She put a hand on her chest. "I was so shocked to see the headlines."

"Then you know that I was allegedly involved in the

scandal," Austin noted. "Surely you don't want someone like me raising money for your charity."

"On the contrary, Austin," Samara replied, shaking
her head. "The Cowboy Auction starts in a few minutes,
and I'm counting on you to be up there onstage with me."

"But what about that story?" Austin insisted. It was
clear to her that he did not want to participate in the
auction and Laney's heart warmed at his efforts, but she
also knew that Samara wouldn't back down.

Samara clutched at his arm. "Not to worry, Austin.
I don't believe a word that the paper said about you. I
have the utmost confidence in your character."

Laney set her mouth in a firm line. "It's me you have
a problem with, isn't that right?"

Samara released Austin and turned to her, glaring.
"No. I already know you're a liar." Laney saw her eyes
flit down to her belly and back up to her face. "You can't
hide the evidence any longer."

Austin put his arm around Laney protectively, but she
shook it off. She would deal with this shark of a woman
on her own terms.

"Speaking of evidence…" Laney's eyes narrowed
suspiciously. "You know what, Samara? Ever since
you've come to Granger, nothing has been the same."

Samara laughed and then purposely lowered her
voice. "And that's a bad thing? Look around you, Laney,"
she said sarcastically. "There hasn't been this much excitement in this crappy little town since… Well…never!"

Laney clenched her jaw and didn't respond. A reporter was hurrying toward them and there was no way
she was going to be caught on camera.

Besides, Samara was right. The town of Granger had
experienced a kind of revitalization that had led to an

increase in tourists, as well as business for the BWB Ranch.

Last summer Laney had kicked things off with all the publicity around her athletic success, and tonight it looked like Samara was going all the way into the end zone for the touchdown.

That didn't mean she had to stick around to watch Samara's celebratory dance. Without another word, Laney stalked away.

Samara watched Laney go and hoped she would never return. From the very beginning, the woman had been nothing but trouble. She was harder to get rid of than a bad movie critic.

"Laney, wait!" Austin called out.

Samara put her hand on his arm to stop him. "Austin, let her go. It's obvious she doesn't want to be with you. Besides, the auction is almost ready to begin."

Austin shook away from her grasp. "I told you, Samara. I'm not for sale."

Samara clicked her tongue against her teeth. "That's a shame. Come with me, I have something to show you."

She led the way to the main ballroom. "Look along the back wall. What do you see there?"

She watched as Austin narrowed his eyes. "Ah... I see you understand now," she cooed. "The entire event is being captured on film to be shown at a later date, of my choosing. There's a lot of interest lately in All-American cowboys, especially wealthy ones like you, who somehow find it in their heart to give back."

"What's the name of the charity?" he asked.

"I haven't decided yet," she snapped, and then immediately softened her tone. "But what does it matter? The media and the public will eat this event up."

Austin leaned against the doorjamb. "This sounds like blackmail, Samara," he ground out in a low voice.

She reached up and playfully adjusted his bowtie. "Call it what you will, but in light of your recent, shall we say, indiscretions, don't you think it's wise to play nice?"

Austin twisted away from her and folded his arms. "I thought you said you didn't believe any of that stuff in the article."

Samara put her hand on her chest. "I don't," she replied innocently. "But other people might. The Cowboy Auction is a way to show the public just how wonderful, honest and incredibly sexy you are." Samara wedged her arm through Austin's and led him away, her eyes gleaming. "Tonight is your chance for vindication."

Chapter 13

Laney emerged from the restroom just in time to see Samara leading Austin away. Tears welled up in her eyes, but she quickly wiped them away, not wanting to call attention to herself. Although she'd heard Austin call out to her, he obviously wasn't too heartbroken that she'd left his side.

True, she'd offered no explanation. Visits to the bathroom were becoming more frequent now that she was in the second trimester of pregnancy. It wasn't something she wanted to call attention to in public, especially in front of a man, let alone Samara Lionne.

She clenched her fists and strode to the entry of the ballroom. Her eyes scanned the room, but there was no sign of Austin or Samara.

There was something about that woman that she didn't like—didn't trust. Cowboy Auction be damned, she thought. There was no way she was going to let Samara, or any other woman for that matter, dig her claws into her man.

Someone tapped her shoulder and she nearly jumped out of her wedge heels.

"Jameson!" Laney turned around and punched him lightly on his biceps.

"Ouch," he said in a mock hurt tone.

"You scared me half to death! Why didn't you announce yourself?"

"That's no fun," Jameson said with a grin.

Brooke gave her a quick hug. "I tried to tell him, Laney, but he insisted on sneaking up on you."

"I used to do that to you all the time when you were little, remember?"

Laney rolled her eyes. "Of course I do. I'd be grooming one of Mama's horses and you'd come up behind me. You'd scare me and the horse. You're lucky you didn't get your butt kicked!"

Jameson waved her comment away. "You're a girl. That never would have happened."

"Not by me. By the horse," Laney replied good-naturedly, turning to Brooke, who was standing right beside him. "You know, if you'd like to get rid of him, you could enter him in the Cowboy Auction," she joked.

Brooke laughed. "I think I'll keep him around for now."

Jameson waggled his eyebrows at the two women. "I heard that it's co-ed this time. Maybe I should see what's available!"

"Don't you dare!" both women cried out, attracting the attention of some onlookers.

Laney adored Brooke and thought that she was a wonderful choice for her brother. And Brooke protested because, like Laney, she didn't want any other woman even thinking they had a chance with her man.

Jameson held his hands up and grinned. "Okay. I know when I've been voted down." He checked his watch. "The auction is going to start any minute. We should probably find our table."

Brooke kissed him on the cheek. "You go on ahead, honey. It's girl-talk time."

The two women laughed as they watched Jameson make a beeline toward the Browards' reserved table, as if he couldn't leave fast enough.

"That's one way to get rid of a man," Laney remarked. She drew Brooke aside. "What's going on?"

"I was wondering the same thing. What changed your mind about attending the ball?"

"This dress and the fact that Austin gave it to me."

Brooke's eyes widened. "He did? It's gorgeous and you look fantastic."

"Thank you, so do you."

"Where is Austin?"

"He's getting ready to be auctioned off."

Brooke's jaw dropped. "Lydia told me that Samara was the grand prize, but I had no idea that Austin was involved."

"Neither did he, apparently. And as far as I know, he's going to go through with it. He and Samara are nowhere to be seen."

"They're probably backstage. Do you want me to go find Lydia and tell her that you're looking for him?"

Laney shook her head. "Don't bother. He'll know soon enough."

Brooke tilted her head. "You're planning something," she stated with a smile.

Laney squared her shoulders and nodded. "Let's just say this will be a night that no one will forget."

Austin peeked his head out from behind the curtain. He spotted Gwen, Steven, Wes and Lydia sitting at a reserved table located near the stage, but Laney wasn't there. His heart suddenly seized in his chest. Had she left the event and returned home?

Was she ill?

He let the curtain fall back in place. There were two other contestants waiting backstage with him. One of them was a farmer he didn't know and the other was Trey, Laney's ranch hand.

They didn't formally greet each other, but Austin knew that Trey remembered him, even though whenever he was over at Laney's house, he barely spoke to him.

"I'm not digging this at all," Austin remarked, forcing the worry out of his voice. "What about you?"

Trey hooked a finger and pulled at his collar. "I didn't have anything else to do tonight." He cracked his knuckles. "Besides, a free meal and a free girl, what more could a man want?"

How about some dignity and self-respect, Austin thought.

"I'm hoping to find a wife," the farmer piped up.

"I've already got one in mind," Austin replied. As soon as the words were out, he regretted them. His matrimonial plans were not meant to be discussed in front of two men he didn't even know.

Trey cracked his knuckles again. "She's a good woman," he said without looking at Austin.

Austin couldn't have agreed more. Laney was Trey's boss, but she was his future. It was up to him to prove that he was the right man for her.

Suddenly, there was a round of applause. Austin heard the mayor of Granger introduce himself and say a few words. A thundering applause was heard and Austin knew that Samara was now onstage.

The curtain rose.

The three men stepped forward.

Austin took a deep breath.

Showtime.

Laney sat next to Brooke at the table reserved for the Browards. Every place setting had a name tag, and in front of every plate there was a small paddle.

Grandpa Charles picked up his paddle. "When I was growing up, these were a lot bigger," he whispered. "I remember when my father—"

Steven cleared his throat. "Dad, now is not the time to relive your disciplinary moments," he interjected in a low voice.

Grandpa Charles sniffed and retorted, "Tell that to my backside!"

All of the Broward men started laughing hysterically.

"Hush!" Gwen reprimanded. "The auction is starting." She looked around the table at Lydia, Brooke and Laney. "Ladies, get your paddles ready."

"I'm the only one who's going to be bidding at this table," Laney announced. "The rest of you are happily taken."

Brooke nudged her with an elbow. "You go, girl. You bid for your man."

Laney smiled. "And I intend to win."

Austin lifted his left hand and shaded his eyes. It was difficult to see under the stage lights, but he had to try. He had to find Laney.

In front of the stage, there was a large dance floor and behind that were the tables, all of which were completely filled. When the curtain had risen, he'd lost sight of the Broward table, but now all he had to do was look for the most beautiful woman in the room.

Seconds later, he spotted her sitting between Brooke and Gwen, and he exhaled in relief. He was too far away so he couldn't see the expression on her face.

But he was glad she hadn't left. She was still there.

And even better. She had a paddle in her hand.

"Ladies and gentlemen," Samara announced, "we have a very exciting evening planned for you all. When I arrived in Granger several months ago, I was so enamored with the story of Wes and Lydia Broward, who first met during your annual Cowboy Auction, that I decided to reprise the event tonight for charity.

"Ladies may bid on their choice of three of Granger's most attractive and eligible bachelors, while the men—" Samara paused dramatically "—may bid on the grand prize—one glorious evening out with me."

The room erupted into a combination of applause, hoots and hollers.

"May the best woman—and man—win," Samara said dramatically.

Squeals of excitement pealed through the air as the first bachelor stepped forward.

"Dylan Tyler is a farmer and a brand-new resident of Granger. He's thirty-three years old, five feet nine inches tall, weighs a hundred and ninety pounds and he loves to ski and watch movies. Sounds like a guy after my own heart. Let's start the bidding at one hundred dollars."

After a slight hesitation, paddles started flipping all over the room as the auctioneer called out the ever-changing price of the gorgeous farmer. It didn't take long for a lucky lady to win Tyler at the closing bid of one thousand dollars.

Next, Samara leaned into the microphone and called out Trey's name. She gave his stats and explained that although he, too, was new in town, he was a pro at managing Laney's stables.

"Break a leg, man," Austin grunted out of the side of his mouth.

Trey stepped forward, but looked back at him and glared, as if he'd been insulted by his comment.

"Bidding for Trey will begin at five hundred dollars. Who wants a date with this handsome hunk who loves horses?"

For a second, recalling how he was unsure what role other than ranch hand that Trey played in her life, Austin feared that Laney would bid for him. But as far as he could tell, under the lights, which were getting hotter by the minute, her paddle remained down.

It took longer for Trey's bidding to be complete, but finally Samara announced that he'd been "sold" for twenty-five hundred dollars to bidder number thirty-five.

"Congratulations, Dr. Kate Simmons. I understand you're Granger's only veterinarian. I'm sure you and Trey will enjoy talking for hours about your love for animals."

Austin glanced quickly over at Samara, who seemed to be really enjoying herself.

Yet it struck him as odd that Samara knew a lot about each contestant and he wondered how she'd come about the information. He knew a lot could be learned from the internet, but these two men were new in town, plus, they didn't strike him as the type to be using Facebook or Tweeting their time away.

"Last, but certainly not least, we have up for auction—Austin Johns. The rules forbade me to bid, otherwise I'd have this delicious man all to myself. Austin hails from Dallas, Texas, and word around town is that he's going to be hitching his horse and riding off into the sunset soon, so ladies, get your paddles ready for this hot multimillionaire. We'll start things rolling with bids of one thousand dollars."

Austin stepped forward and his eyes caught hers, or at least he thought they did. But even though he was in a different position onstage, he still couldn't see her face too clearly. Worse, the paddle he'd seen in her hand previously was no longer there.

There were butterflies in his stomach as the bidding started. Slowly at first, and then to Austin's amazement, it quickly gained momentum. Paddles were flipping all across the room, waved in the air by women young and old. The bid amount quickly escalated to ten thousand dollars.

Suddenly, Laney's paddle shot up and his heart beat faster as he realized that she must have hidden it on her lap. Austin grinned as she held it high and steady in the air. "Can I get fifteen thousand dollars for this young man? Going once, going twice…" the auctioneer cried out.

A roar went through the crowd as a paddle in the back went up, but Austin couldn't see who held it.

"Fifteen thousand dollars! Can I get twenty thousand dollars for Mr. Austin Johns?"

"How does fifty thousand dollars sound?"

"Miss Broward," exclaimed the auctioneer. "Fifty thousand dollars? This is unprecedented. Are you sure?"

Laney got up from her seat and walked onto the dance floor, the paddle held high in her left hand.

She looked up at Austin onstage and their eyes met. "I've never been more sure of anything in my life."

Laney smiled and turned back to face the audience, her paddle held high and her baby bump front and center for all to see. Austin's heart swelled with pride at her courage and lack of fear.

"I bid fifty thousand dollars for Mr. Austin Johns!"

"Going once, going twice...sold to Miss Laney Broward."

The crowd erupted in raucous applause while Austin made his way offstage toward Laney. He gave her a quick embrace when what he really wanted to do was kiss her. "Are you crazy?" he whispered in her ear. "Fifty thousand for me?"

She smiled and laid her warm hand against his cheek. "Are you saying you're not worth it?"

He pulled her even closer. "You know I am, but what I want to know is why?"

Laney grabbed his hand and led him away. "Not now. We have to go back to our seats. It's time for Samara's auction."

Chapter 14

Backstage, Samara watched Austin embrace Laney on the dance floor as jealousy lit her insides on fire. She would have liked to have someone as gorgeous and kind as Austin for herself. But it was clear he only had eyes for Laney.

"Here's your mirror, Samara," Lydia said, who'd just arrived to help. "I know how important it is for you to look your best."

Samara grabbed the object from her former assistant. "So nice of you to show up for my event, Lydia."

Lydia didn't even flinch. She was used to Samara's outbursts. "I wanted to see for myself," she responded quietly. "I can't believe you're still in Granger."

"When I said I was committed to being here, I meant it. Now that I have Wes's property, I'm in negotiation with Meredith Palmer to buy her half of the Palmer Ranch."

"I had no idea."

"Yes, I've offered her an insane amount of money to buy the place, far more than it's worth, but the woman hasn't even budged yet. She told me that your future brother-in-law, Jameson Broward, wants it, too."

Lydia shook her head. "I don't know, Samara. Maybe she's not interested in selling."

Samara laughed and handed the mirror back to Lydia.

"Darling, how naive can you be? Everyone has a price. Even your soon-to-be husband. You better go back to your seat. It's time for the main event."

Lydia backed away, inwardly thankful that she was no longer working for Samara, glad that she'd removed herself from having to deal with the vengeful look that always seemed to be present in the movie star's eyes. As she hurried back to the Browards' table, she wondered who would be Samara's next victim.

Through a slight gap in the curtain, Samara peeked out at her invited guests, at the media that were recording her every move tonight and finally, her eyes settled on the Broward family.

The day had finally arrived. The moment she'd been waiting for her entire life.

A deep murmur rumbled through the crowd as Samara pushed back the curtain and took to the stage again.

This is for you, Momma.

Gwendolyn patted her husband on the arm. "Don't think for one second that you will be lifting that paddle," she warned.

Steven caught her hand and kissed the ridge of his wife's knuckles. "I already know what it's like to sleep on the barn floor. I don't want to spend the rest of my life there," he joked.

"Hush, you two lovebirds," Laney admonished, jerking her chin toward the stage. "She's about to say something."

Samara cleared her throat and adjusted the microphone.

"First, I'd like to thank all the fine people of Granger for their hospitality toward me these past few months. I'd always heard that small towns were welcoming, but I really didn't believe it until I came to live here. I have truly felt welcomed. There's a simplicity here and an innate goodness that I find extremely humbling, and coming from L.A., I probably needed a good dose of both. And for that, I thank you."

The crowd responded by applauding and there were a few catcall whistles, too.

"But I did find a few similarities between Granger and my life in Hollywood, where things aren't always as they seem. And people aren't always as honest as they claim to be."

She paused again, waiting until she could feel the suspense building in the room, until all eyes were upon her. "There is one person in this town whom I feel it is my duty to expose. One person who has been fooling you all for years. His name is Steven Broward."

Samara smiled inwardly as a crescendo of alarm rolled through the crowd and some people started murmuring amongst themselves. She waited until the room was quiet and began to speak again.

"Steven Broward is a liar and a phony." She gestured toward the Browards' table. "This so-called devoted family man, whom you all know as one of Montana's most upstanding citizens, abandoned one of his children without remorse."

To the people in the audience, it seemed as though Samara was glaring at every person sitting at the Broward table, but her stare was only meant for one.

Gwen could feel Samara's eyes on their table. She glanced over at her husband, fright in her eyes, and grabbed his arm. "What's going on, Steven? What's Samara talking about?"

Steven couldn't look at her. He could only stare back at the woman onstage, at this person who had insinuated such terrible things about him. Things that weren't true. He felt chilled to the bone at her accusations.

His lips quivered. "I have no idea."

He broke away from his wife and his body twisted in his seat. It seemed as if all eyes in the ballroom were fixated on him. He'd always been a quiet man, an introvert, and always shunned the spotlight.

Now Samara had drawn him into some kind of sick web, and he wanted desperately to get out, but he didn't know how.

Steven twisted back and faced his family. Wes, Jameson and Laney all had questions in their eyes, but they were waiting for him to get his head together. They knew their father well enough to know that he needed time to gather his thoughts.

He loved them all so much. Jameson for his staunch loyalty to the ranch, Wes for his innovative mind and Laney for her courage and ambition.

They were all his, born as the result of the intense love for his wife, Gwen. A love that, because of the nature of their arranged marriage, had taken a while to bloom but had fully blossomed.

He didn't want to lose her now.

Steven grabbed Gwen's hand and squeezed it, for into the cloud of his thoughts, Samara's voice struck through.

"I am Steven Broward's daughter," she announced. "I am the one he abandoned."

Her words nearly knocked the breath out of his lungs.

What was she talking about? He had only one daughter, Laney.

Steven looked up to the stage, at the woman glaring down at him, and finally, he could take no more. He stood up in his place, nearly causing his chair to fall over and clenched his hands into fists.

"This is insane. You're lying," he said, hardly believing the savageness in his voice. But he couldn't help it. This woman seemed bent on not only destroying him, but everything he and his father and grandfather before him had built.

Gwen pulled on his tuxedo jacket. "Sit down, honey. Don't play into her games."

"I can assure you that this is not a game, Mrs. Broward," Samara responded in a snide tone. "I was conceived thirty-four years ago, just before you and your husband married. My mother's name was Georgia Jackson."

Steven felt the blood drain from his face.

Georgia Jackson. His first love.

He hadn't thought about her in years. But suddenly the memories started flowing back. Her body, thin and lean like the dancer she'd wanted to be, and her voice as deep and as sexy as Eartha Kitt's, and all the nights he'd stolen away from the ranch just to be with her.

His father and mother had not approved of Georgia. They'd never said the words, but he'd known they'd thought she was "common." Georgia had stars in her eyes and her feet pointed straight toward Broadway.

Much as he'd tried to hide their relationship, her parents must have known about it. Back then, Granger was even smaller than it was today and rumors traveled like tumbleweeds. They'd wanted him to marry a woman more suitable, someone who loved ranching as much as he did, and although he'd loved Georgia, he was young enough to succumb to the pressures of his family.

So, he'd broken up with his first love and began pursuing Gwendolyn, who came from a wealthy family just like he did. Georgia promptly left town and was never heard from again.

Steven felt Gwen's hand clutch at his arm and his throat worked nervously. He had no idea what to say to her or to his children.

"My mother told me that she was Steven's first love. He had sex with her, then he broke her heart by abandoning her and marrying you," Samara said, leaning into the microphone, her voice dripping with venom.

She continued to address Gwen. "How does it feel to come in second?"

"That's enough, Samara!" Steven shouted, vaguely aware that cameras and likely smartphones, too, were capturing his every word. "I'll not have you speaking to my wife that way!"

Steven glanced down at Gwen, whose eyes were filling with tears. He could only imagine what was going through her mind right now. Although he'd been honest with Gwen about his parents' wishes from the start, he'd never really discussed his relationship with Georgia.

Gwen pulled her hand away. "Is what she saying true, Steven?"

He leaned over the table, so he could get a closer view at Samara. She had Georgia's thin yet curvy body and medium skin tone. He couldn't see what color her eyes were, but when he really looked at her, he saw that she was the spitting image of her mother.

Thankfully, she didn't have much of his physical

traits, save for the angularity of her jaw, and perhaps the same stubbornness of will.

"It's true that there was a woman in my life before you, Gwen. Her name was Georgia, but I had no idea Georgia was pregnant when we broke up."

And in the years since, she had not once contacted him. He'd had no way of knowing that he had another child out there.

"You're lying!" Samara raged, so loudly that feedback from the microphone rang throughout the room.

"How can I be lying about something I had no knowledge about?" he shouted back. "She never said one word to me."

"And if she had? What would you have done?"

Steven looked around and saw the eyes of his friends, neighbors and business associates staring back at him. Every one of them looked absolutely stunned at what they were hearing. At that moment, he felt so much pressure and so much defeat that all he wanted to do was shrink back into his seat.

"Truthfully?" Steven responded, with much less fervor. "I don't know."

He did know one thing. His parents would have been supremely disappointed in him. He turned to his father, lowered his voice and whispered, "Dad? What should I do?"

"This all sounds like a bunch of Hollywood mumbo-jumbo to me," Grandpa Charles snarled, loud enough for everyone in the room to hear. "She's trying to make us Browards look like a bunch of country hicks in front of all these cameras."

"I'm telling the truth," Samara insisted, although her voice had lost a little of its urgency.

Gwen picked up on her change in tone, and she suddenly stood and locked arms in solidarity with her husband. "Prove it."

"How dare you challenge me?" Samara raged.

She glared at the woman who had stolen her mother's only true love. Her mother had never really admitted it, but she knew that when Steven had left her broken-hearted, weary and pregnant, that she had never really recovered.

Samara held back tears. The Browards were her enemies. No way was she going to admit defeat by crying. "My mother was so beautiful and so graceful in her youth, and you both stole it from her!" In a strange way, it pleased Samara that Gwen wasn't particularly good-looking, but she did have a regal way about her, as if she knew more than her face held. It hardly mattered; where Gwen failed in the looks department, she still had her wealth, power and status in the Granger community.

But not for long, Samara vowed to herself.

Jameson spoke up in defense of his father. "Nothing you've said here tonight makes one bit of sense."

Samara put one hand on her hip and lasered a gaze at the man who was her main competition for the Palmer Ranch. "Isn't that just like a Broward? Always trying to make believe that only their opinions count, that their word is god, and unless you can prove you're worth something to them, you're branded a nobody," she sneered. "That's what Steven and his parents thought about my mother. They thought she was a nobody and that's why he broke her heart!"

Steven hung his head, knowing that her words were true.

"Why doesn't someone just pull the plug on that microphone so she'll shut up?" suggested Jameson in a low voice.

"Hush," Brooke said, jabbing him in the side with her elbow.

"No. Let her speak," Gwen urged. "We're still waiting to hear what proof she has that she is Steven's daughter."

"My mother told me that my father was dead," Samara began.

"There! You see!" Jameson exclaimed, pointing a finger at her. "That proves that she is the one who is lying."

"It proves nothing," Samara retorted, "except for the fact that my mother didn't want me to know what kind of a father I had. She didn't want me to know that he'd abandoned her and ultimately, abandoned me.

"I grew up with nothing," Samara continued in dramatic fashion, unshed tears welling up in her eyes. "We lived on food stamps while my mother worked menial jobs. She could never afford to go to college. She worked two jobs most years, and tried to be with me as much as she could. But I was often alone while she was working, trying to provide for us. Not once did she go on a date or entertain a man," Samara cried out. "She took care of me. She loved me."

"Why didn't Georgia ever contact me?" Steven asked.

"Did you ever try to get in touch with her?" Samara fired back.

"No, but that was because I was already involved with Gwen. We were going to be married. It wouldn't have been right."

Samara shook her head, and her tone was vicious. "I'm tired of hearing your lame excuses. My mother is dead." She watched without pity as Steven shook his head in disbelief. "She passed away when I was a teen-

ager, having worked herself into an early grave. While
you and your wife had everything. We had nothing. No
support at all."

Samara made her way down the stage and walked
over to the table.

"You say you want proof. I have it right here."

She unclasped a necklace that was hidden behind the
giant diamond one around her neck, and held it before
Steven, dangling it like a hypnotist.

"This is the first and only gift you gave to my mother.
It was the only thing she ever had that had any value."

Steven thrust out his hand. "Let me see that," he
barked.

Samara placed it gingerly into his cupped palm, without touching him.

Steven's eyes widened at the sight of the tiny pair of
solid twenty-four-karat gold ballet slippers. He remembered the night he'd given it to Georgia, in recognition
of her dream to be a dancer and in celebration of his
love for her. It was that night that Samara must have
been conceived.

At the look on Steven's face, Samara said, "You remember, don't you?"

No one spoke and the cameras continued to roll as
the Broward family and everyone in the room waited
for Steven's response.

"Did you give that necklace to Georgia?" Gwen asked
quietly.

"Y-yes," he stammered, closing his fist around the
jewelry that held so many memories for him. "Yes, I
did." His eyes slid shut for a moment.

What have I done?

Gwen slowly sank back into her seat. "So it is true," she muttered in disbelief.

Her husband had a child with another woman.

A woman he had wooed and bedded and loved far earlier than he'd known Gwen.

She thought her marriage was strong, but was it strong enough to withstand this?

Wes spoke up. "How do you know it's the same necklace? It could be a fake."

Steven shook his head. "It's not. There's not another one in the world like this one. I had it custom-made in Bozeman for Georgia. See, her initials are there. One letter is engraved on each shoe."

"Let me see the necklace, son," said Grandpa Charles.

He handed it to his father, who examined it closely. Then he handed it back. "And you'd told me you spent your entire allowance savings on fishing tackle."

One more secret was out and Steven hung his head in shame. "I'm sorry, Dad."

He handed the necklace back to Samara, being careful not to make physical contact with her.

Samara took it and reclasped it around her neck, and dropped the diamond one over it. "I'm the one you should be apologizing to. I'm the one you left with nothing. I'm the one who grew up without a father!"

But Steven could not respond. His reputation and everything he'd staked his life on was in danger of being destroyed because of a secret, and now that it was out, he didn't know what do next. He threw his arm across his eyes and slunk even farther down into his seat as Wes, Jameson and Laney stared in wonder at a possible half sister.

Chapter 15

Nobody moved. The ballroom was hot-wired with tension as the partygoers waited to see what would happen next. Even the waiters, who had begun to serve the meal, were now leaning against the walls, holding trays of food in front of them.

No one could have foretold this unexpected turn of events, and the auction for a one-night "date" with Samara seemed long forgotten.

Rooted to her seat in disbelief, Laney felt as if she was floating in a bubble of suspended animation or that the Browards were the punchline of somebody's idea of a very sick joke. Her family seemed frozen in an awful nightmare and nobody knew how to end it, least of all her parents.

The entire reputation of the Broward family, and possibly their livelihood, was at risk, and at the moment, she could see that Gwen and Steven were too shocked to even fight back.

Samara's necklace was like an invisible noose of truth. Sure, it wasn't accurate or scientific like a paternity test, yet it was cloaked in emotion. For what it represented was love and passion and hope. And what is a truer end result of all that than a child?

The gold necklace was a gift given in secret, much like the child that was conceived. Both were subsequently hidden for years.

But why tell us this news now? Laney thought.

She had watched Samara closely throughout the entire ordeal, on the hunt for any signs of Hollywood phoniness in her speech and demeanor. And despite her less than positive feelings about the A-list movie star, she had also tried to listen to her tirade with open ears.

Now Samara was standing before the Broward family table. But, amazingly, for the first time that evening, she'd turned away from the cameras.

Shoulders hunched over, head bowed, crying, the sound on the cusp of a howl. Samara was no longer a movie star preening for a ten-second sound bite, she was a secret daughter mourning the loss of a father she never knew.

Laney's heart suddenly seized in her chest. That's when she knew that this was no act. Samara's pain was real, and if what she'd said about her father was true, so terribly unnecessary.

She wasn't about to allow another secret to destroy her family. Laney took a deep breath and scooted her chair back. Austin caught her lightly by the wrist.

"Where are you going?" he asked.

"I'm going to hug my half sister."

She shook away from his well-meaning grasp and stood. It seemed as if a thousand eyes were pressed into her back as she made her way around the table.

A murmur went through the crowd. Those that hadn't already been live-Tweeting the event started anew, however most just inched forward in their seats and craned their necks to get a better view.

Cameramen rechecked their equipment to ensure there would be no technical glitches in their continued coverage of this unusual event. But if you asked them privately or brought them a beer or two, they'd tell you that they thought Samara was on the kooky side of Sane Street. Their advice? Always cross to the other side of the road.

Gwen and Steven looked at one another and back at their only daughter, round with their first grandchild. Laney was so beautiful and usually so predictable. Her decisions were meted out with much thought and precision. But now she moved hastily toward Samara, as if her entire life depended upon it.

Laney put a hand on Samara's shoulder and didn't feel the least bit offended when the woman shrank away. She simply waited until the actress turned around to face her.

Samara's makeup was smeared and she looked a mess, and Laney felt a surge of pity.

"No child should grow up without a father," Laney said. "I'm so sorry you didn't get a chance to know our dad because if you had, you would know he's a good man. He would never knowingly walk away and abandon one of his own. Not ever."

Samara swiped at one eye. "You're just saying that because you're his daughter," she sniffled.

"No, I'm saying that because it's true and because you're his daughter, too."

She turned to Steven and she saw that his eyes had filled with tears. "And no father should be denied a relationship with his child."

Laney reached for Samara's hand, and she was surprised when the star took it tentatively, before grasping it tightly.

"Several weeks ago, my family and I made a pact. We vowed to never let secrets destroy our special bond, a love that has carried forth throughout generations, and we won't let it happen today. Especially since it appears we now have a new Broward in the family and soon—" Laney patted her tummy "—another one on the way."

She turned, gazed at Austin and continued. "I am blessed to have Austin Johns, the father of my baby, in my life. Although I am sorry to say that it took me a while to realize what a lucky woman I am. I'll never again take him for granted, nor the love of each member of my family."

Finally, she addressed the audience. "Let's all remember the root of who we are is our relationship with our loved ones. Our mothers and our fathers, sisters and brothers, grandparents, aunts and uncles and cousins. We must all be willing to restore the broken hearts and forgive the broken promises. So that the love that links us all will be forever strengthened for generations to come."

The stunned silence that had filled the room was now replaced with a burst of applause.

Laney didn't know if the cameras were still rolling or not and she didn't care. She was just glad that the truth was out and in a way she was grateful for Samara's outburst, because it made her realize how close she'd come to losing Austin and breaking her own child's heart.

When Laney dropped Samara's hand and hugged her, she did not return the heartfelt gesture. Instead she stiffened in her arms, unable to feel joy, unable to feel anything but confusion at Laney's empathy.

The applause continued. For once, Samara didn't care if it wasn't meant for her. All she wanted to do was feel something in her heart besides rage and hurt. Was that even possible anymore?

"It's okay now," Laney said, her face close to Samara's cheek. "We believe you."

Samara didn't respond, for what could she say? Laney's voice was clear, unlike Samara's conscience. When she'd made the decision to move to Granger, she never could have imagined things would turn out this way.

Steven watched Laney embrace Samara, and his heart tightened in his chest. He'd never been so proud of his daughter than he was right now. While he'd sat there in a state of shock, she'd taken the lead in trying to salvage a disgraceful situation and turn it into the beginning of a new relationship.

His chin dropped and he shook his head slowly, afraid to look at Gwen. Did she believe him when he'd told Samara, told the whole world in front of those godforsaken cameras, that he hadn't known Georgia was pregnant?

He felt her hand clasp his and his head snapped up, although he was afraid to see her soft brown eyes.

At one time, they'd been the eyes of a stranger. A woman he'd practically been forced to marry for the sake of good breeding and maintaining the wealth of their respective families. But now, after thirty-four years of marriage and three children, Steven could honestly say Gwen was his best friend. All he wanted now was her forgiveness.

"I'm sorry," he mouthed, knowing full well she deserved much more than two simple words. She deserved an explanation, but he had none to give.

Gwen squeezed his hand. "Go to her. We'll talk later."

Tears smarting his eyes, Steven swallowed hard and then half stumbled out of his chair.

Laney released Samara from her embrace, while Steven stood there, unsure what to do next. He stuck both hands in his tuxedo pockets, and just as quickly took them out again. He ran his thumb along the inside of his left hand, over the round edge of his wedding ring, taking strength in the fact that it was still on his finger.

Steven was a man known for the brevity of his words. Folks who knew him best would say that he liked to graze upon his thoughts before sharing them. He was never in a hurry. Yet right now, he had a ton of things he wanted to say, but he knew that no words could describe the jumble of emotions he was feeling, nor would they bring back all the lost years.

"If I'd known about you, I—I would have welcomed you with open arms," he stammered awkwardly.

He started to put his hands in his pockets again. Seconds later, he changed his mind and reached for his newfound daughter. But her shoulders folded inward and she shied away from him, pulling his heart away with her.

Up close now, Steven could see even more the resemblance to her mother, Georgia. Samara was as beautiful as she had once been. He could see her thin arms trembling and her eyes shifting toward him warily, as if she wasn't sure whether he was going to attack her or hug her. This saddened him, almost as much as not knowing she had existed.

Samara fought back more tears as she took another step away from her father, ignoring the need to dive right into his arms.

She'd waited so long for this moment. For years, she'd practiced all the words she would say if she ever met her father. She'd never quite believed her mother when she'd told her he was dead. He was alive in her imagination every day…and now, he was close enough to hug.

Still, it felt strange to be standing here in front of the man who'd unwittingly caused her and her mother so much pain.

Her mind flashed back to the night of her eighteenth birthday, when she'd come home from a date and found her mother dead. At first, she'd thought she was only sleeping, the chamomile tea she drank to calm her nerves was nearly empty. But when she wouldn't wake up, Samara screamed and screamed until her next door neighbor called the police. From that day forward, Samara was alone.

But not for long.

She wasn't stupid. She'd figured out fairly young that her body and her beauty could be used to fill the gaps in her heart with adoration from men, money and Hollywood.

She was a star! Her glamorous life was coveted by millions worldwide, fans longed to be in her presence, while her own father had abandoned her without looking back.

Or so she had always thought.

The irony was she'd spent months planning to ruin the Browards, but her "victory" had imploded in a matter of minutes.

The clapping had stopped, but she wasn't sure when. Suddenly, she realized that the entire ballroom was silent, seemingly waiting for her next move, her next line.

Perhaps they believed this was part of the ball, some hokey on-the-spot drama she'd dreamed up for ratings.

But no, she wasn't acting and she wasn't playing games anymore.

She regarded the rest of the Broward family, and thought how perfectly they represented all that she'd ever wanted, but never had. Who was she kidding? She would never fit in with them. At that moment, a knot of emotion welled in her throat and she burst into tears and fled from the room.

Jameson and Wes looked at each other in disbelief. They actually had a half sister! Both of them could hardly believe it.

"Do you think she's gone for good?" Jameson asked, not caring if his tone sounded harsh.

"Honey! I'm surprised at you," Brooke exclaimed. "Even though it's obvious she was playing to the cameras."

Steven trudged back to the table. "Everything Samara said was true," he said ruefully.

Wes guffawed. "Dad, you can't really believe that Samara Lionne is your daughter? I mean, no offense, but she looks nothing like you."

Lydia elbowed her fiancé. "That's not nice."

Even though she knew that Wes and his father joked around all the time, Samara was her old boss. Despite her quirkiness, Lydia did care about her.

"But Samara did have the necklace that her mother gave her," Brooke pointed out.

"It's probably a fake," Jameson said, not ready to believe that it wasn't.

Steven sat down. "Like I said earlier, I can assure you it's not a fake, son. It's the same one that I gave her all those years ago."

He rubbed his hand along his temple. "Lord, if I had only known!"

Laney came around and put her hands on her mother's shoulders. "If you had known about Samara, would you still have married Mom?"

His eyes lifted and sank into Gwen's. The private knowing look they shared was the result of years of love and mutual respect.

He touched her hand and when he spoke, his voice was choked with emotion. "Yes, I would have married you. In fact, I wouldn't change a thing."

Gwen leaned over and kissed her husband gently on the lips. "Let's go home and talk this through over a plate of my cookies. I made your favorite this afternoon—chocolate chip!"

"That sounds wonderful," he said as they both stood. "Why don't you all join us?"

"But don't you want to talk about it alone?" Jameson asked.

Gwen shook her head. "Remember our pact. No more secrets. We'll discuss it with all of us together."

Everyone else got up and started to walk away, all except Laney, who hung back.

Gwen turned abruptly. "Are you coming with us?"

"I'll be along soon. I have something I need to discuss with Austin."

Gwen nodded and gave Laney and Austin a knowing smile. "We'll keep the cookies warm. For both of you."

She linked hands with Steven and walked out of the ballroom with her head held high. True, her heart was bruised, but it was still intact, strengthened from years of faithfully loving one man.

A secret can destroy a family, Gwen thought, but it

can also bring one closer together, and she knew that no matter what, the Browards would prevail.

Laney plopped down in a chair next to Austin, suddenly exhausted.

"Are you okay?" Austin asked.

She blew out a breath and nodded. "Just overwhelmed by everything that happened tonight."

He leaned one elbow on the table and regarded her. "You were amazing with Samara. After everything she said about your father, you still found it in your heart to reach out. How did you do it?"

Laney turned to him. "All I had to do was think about how our child would feel if she never knew her father. I would never want our baby to experience that kind of pain."

He reached for her hand and kissed it gently. "It took a lot for you to admit I was the father of your baby in public. What made you do it?"

"Other than fifty thousand bucks?" she asked and they both erupted in laughter.

She giggled when Austin pulled her onto his lap. And when the laughter had ended, her tone became serious, and she'd never felt more confident in her life.

"The truth is...I love you, Austin. I love you and I love that you are the father of my baby."

Austin placed one hand on her cheek and tilted her chin up. "I love you, too, Laney Broward."

He kissed her fully and deeply, and she squirmed in his lap with delight.

When the kiss ended, he reached into an inside pocket of his tuxedo and pulled out a small velvet box.

Laney's heart beat faster when he put it in her hand.

"Go ahead," he urged. "Open it."

She took the box and slowly cracked it open. Inside was the most ridiculously large and incredibly beautiful diamond ring she'd ever seen.

Her eyes were glued on the huge gem. "Oh, my goodness, this must have cost you a fortune," she blurted out, before she realized that was one of the most unromantic things she could say.

"Let's just call it a return on your investment," Austin chuckled. "Laney, will you marry me?"

Tears of happiness sprang to her eyes and she wrapped her arms around his neck. "I was just waiting for you to ask."

Austin looked deeply into her eyes as he gently ran his hand over her round belly, then he found her lips and gave her his heart.

Epilogue

A few days later, the entire Broward clan was sitting in the kitchen at the BWB Ranch. While the mood was happy, it was also slightly subdued because of the fact that Samara was there, too.

She had been invited by Gwen, who, to the amazement of everyone, had shown an incredible amount of compassion to the movie star that many didn't think she deserved.

Earlier that hour, Samara had confessed that she was the sole cause of the recent trouble in Granger, including all the land that was being mysteriously bought. She'd acted as "The Cobra," the blackmailer who'd taken money from Laney and had leaked her pregnancy to the tabloids. To top it off, she'd even orchestrated the accusations of Austin manipulating Laney's athletic achievements.

"Thank you for not pressing charges," Samara said in a stunned voice. She looked down at the floor and picked at her long nails. "I know you have more than enough grounds to sue me." She lifted her head and said in an unsteady voice, "But as we agreed, I promise I'll get counseling so I can finally get my life and my emotions under control."

"I still don't understand why you did all those things," Wes said. "Why were you so hell-bent on hurting us?"

Samara paused and gestured toward them. "I wanted what you all have, and what you probably take for granted every day." Her voice was raw and choked with emotion. "I wanted a family to love me. It's all I ever cared about. I'm just sorry I went about getting it in the wrong way."

Steven walked over and embraced Samara, and his heart welled up in his chest when this time she did not pull away. "I'm sorry about everything. I promise I'll make it up to you. At least I can try. If you'll let me," he added.

Samara nodded, threw her arms around his neck and the tears began to flow again. "I'd like that very much."

"You're always welcome here at the ranch," Gwen said, watching her husband. She knew it would continue to be difficult to accept Samara's existence, but she had to try, for the sake of her family. All the Browards agreed: Samara had suffered enough. It was time to move on.

"What's going to happen with all the land you bought up around Granger?" Jameson asked.

"Most of it I'm going to return, except for the ranch I bought from Wes," she said, turning in his direction. "If it's okay, I'd like to turn that into a summer camp and retreat for children who have lost their parents."

"It's your land now," Wes grunted. "You can do whatever you'd like with it." Steven and Gwen nodded in agreement.

"That's a wonderful idea!" Brooke exclaimed.

Samara smiled shyly. "I hear you are a wonderful

artist. Perhaps you would consider teaching a pottery class there someday?"

Brooke grinned. She'd always wanted to share her love for art with others. "I'd love to."

Samara turned to Jameson. "And I've decided to back out of the deal to purchase Meredith's half of the Palmer Ranch. Besides, I hear you love ranching a whole lot more than I do."

Jameson nodded gravely in appreciation, as he breathed an inward sigh of relief that the land would become part of the Browards' vast empire. He couldn't wait to sit down with his father and plan how to best utilize it.

"Well, good," Grandpa Charles said. "Maybe now things will get back to normal around here." He reached for a cookie. "Be even better if we saw more of Wes in jeans working the land, rather than in a suit and tie playing on that high-tech phone."

Everyone laughed.

"No can do, Grandpa," Wes said, draping an arm over his fiancée's shoulder. "Lydia and I are heading to Los Angeles permanently. We've decided to launch our own entertainment company."

"Yes, thanks to the contacts I have from when I was working with Samara, we're confident we can build our client base fairly quickly," said Lydia.

Steven felt immediate sadness at the news, but refused to allow disappointment to well up inside him. He quickly released Samara and went over to Wes and shook his hand.

"So you've finally decided to chase Hollywood sharks instead of Granger cattle. I'm sorry to see you go, but I wish you both much luck and success."

With an equally heavy heart, Gwen drifted over and hugged her firstborn son. She was happy that he'd finally discovered his dreams and had the courage to pursue them, but she wished it wasn't so hard to let go.

Wes hugged his parents back. "Look on the bright side, L.A. is beautiful year-round."

"We expect you all to come visit," Lydia added.

"Where do I sign up?" said Grandpa Charles. "I love Montana, but the winter is brutal on these old bones."

"Nobody better go anywhere for the next few months," Laney commanded.

"Why, are you going to hold us hostage?" Wes taunted.

"If that's what it takes to get you to come to a wedding, then yes!" She laughed.

"Whose wedding?" Grandpa Charles demanded in a light tone.

Austin squeezed Laney's hand. "Ours. Laney and I are getting married, as soon as possible."

Lydia and Brooke squealed with delight, and even Samara looked pleased.

Gwen released Wes so she could hug her daughter. "That's wonderful, Laney. I'm so happy for you both."

Austin took turns shaking hands and exchanging high fives with Steven, Wes and Jameson.

"Now you can show your family the ring you've been hiding," Austin said.

Laney twisted the huge rock from where it had been nestled against her palm and flashed it in front of everyone.

"Woot, woot!" she cried, to the oohs and aahs of the women.

"What about me?" Grandpa Charles asked in a playfully brusque tone. "I'm getting married, too! I may not have a huge rock on my hand, but don't I deserve some attention around here?"

Wes and Jameson did a double take. "Grandpa! Get out of here," said Jameson. "Who is she?"

"Miss Polly Ann Wier, if you must know." He scratched his chin. "She's taken quite a shine to me these past few months and, well, I decided I'm not too old to get hitched."

Steven laughed and shook his head in amusement. His father had met Polly Ann as a result of a cowboy auction held a few months ago. His mother had passed away three years earlier and he knew the kind woman had been a much-needed ray of sunshine in his dad's life. "Why, you old devil!" he remarked, a smile of pure happiness on his face.

Grandpa Charles spread his arms wide and pumped out his chest. "Son, if you've still got it, you can still flaunt it," he cackled. "Now, where're my hugs?"

All the women in the room flocked to the Broward patriarch in a group embrace.

"Wow! Two weddings, a baby on the way and a new sister," Laney exclaimed. "Whoever said life in Granger was boring?"

* * * * *

We hope you enjoyed meeting the Broward family.
Next month, don't miss Harmony Evans's
new book, WHEN MORNING COMES,
coming from Harlequin Kimani Romance,
and available at your local bookstore or e-tailer!

A sizzling new miniseries set in the wide-open spaces of Montana!

THE BROWARDS OF MONTANA
Passionate love in the West

JACQUELIN THOMAS	DARA GIRARD	HARMONY EVANS

WRANGLING WES	**ENGAGING BROOKE**	**LOVING LANEY**
Available April 2014	*Available May 2014*	*Available June 2014*

REQUEST YOUR FREE BOOKS!

2 FREE NOVELS
PLUS 2 FREE GIFTS!

KIMANI™
ROMANCE

Love's ultimate destination!

YES! Please send me 2 FREE Harlequin® Kimani™ Romance novels and my 2 FREE gifts (gifts are worth about $10). After receiving them, if I don't wish to receive any more books, I can return the shipping statement marked "cancel." If I don't cancel, I will receive 4 brand-new novels every month and be billed just $5.19 per book in the U.S. or $5.74 per book in Canada. That's a savings of at least 20% off the cover price. It's quite a bargain! Shipping and handling is just 50¢ per book in the U.S. and 75¢ per book in Canada.* I understand that accepting the 2 free books and gifts places me under no obligation to buy anything. I can always return a shipment and cancel at any time. Even if I never buy another book, the two free books and gifts are mine to keep forever.

168/368 XDN F4XC

Name _____
(PLEASE PRINT)

Address _____ Apt. #

City _____ State/Prov. _____ Zip/Postal Code

Signature (if under 18, a parent or guardian must sign)

Mail to the Harlequin® Reader Service:
IN U.S.A.: P.O. Box 1867, Buffalo, NY 14240-1867
IN CANADA: P.O. Box 609, Fort Erie, Ontario L2A 5X3

Want to try two free books from another line?
Call 1-800-873-8635 or visit www.ReaderService.com.

* Terms and prices subject to change without notice. Prices do not include applicable taxes. Sales tax applicable in N.Y. Canadian residents will be charged applicable taxes. Offer not valid in Quebec. This offer is limited to one order per household. Not valid for current subscribers to Harlequin® Kimani™ Romance books. All orders subject to credit approval. Credit or debit balances in a customer's account(s) may be offset by any other outstanding balance owed by or to the customer. Please allow 4 to 6 weeks for delivery. Offer available while quantities last.

Your Privacy—The Harlequin® Reader Service is committed to protecting your privacy. Our Privacy Policy is available online at www.ReaderService.com or upon request from the Harlequin Reader Service.

We make a portion of our mailing list available to reputable third parties that offer products we believe may interest you. If you prefer that we not exchange your name with third parties, or if you wish to clarify or modify your communication preferences, please visit us at www.ReaderService.com/consumerchoice or write to us at Harlequin Reader Service Preference Service, P.O. Box 9062, Buffalo, NY 14269. Include your complete name and address.

KROM13R